Barlow in Charge

After a dozen years as BBC Television's leading detective, Charlie Barlow makes his first appearance in a novel – investigating blackmail in television. But this fascinating and authentically vivid excursion behind the cameras is only the start of an exciting trail which takes the bluff, burly, and belligerent Barlow down the corridors of power in Whitehall; and out into the middle of a sinister and explosive situation which taxes all his ingenuity and resourcefulness. This is Barlow at his most devious, his most efficient, and his most determined.

Elwyn Jones brings to this new Barlow adventure the taut realism and compelling human interest for which his television scripts are famous.

Barlow In Charge

Elwyn Jones

Arthur Barker Limited London

First published in 1973 by
Arthur Barker Limited
11 St John's Hill, London SW11

ISBN 0 213 16425 6

Printed in Great Britain by
Willmer Brothers Limited, Birkenhead

For Euros, my brother

Author's Note

Troy Kennedy Martin first created the character of Detective Chief Inspector Barlow for the original *Z Cars* series. This, the first independent Barlow novel, is published by arrangement with him and with the BBC, and with grateful acknowledgement to Stratford Johns who 'created' Barlow in another sense and who still sustains and extends the character.

PART I

I

Detective Chief Superintendent Charles Barlow was watching television and not because he wanted to. Indeed, the programme was of the sort he normally went to great lengths to avoid. It was one of those earnest inquiries into yet another 'problem of our time'; one of those that invariably ended with stern exhortations to 'face up to our responsibilities' and do something about drug addicts, homeless families, gypsies, unemployed school-leavers, or ill-treated tortoises.

All over the country the people of Britain whose conscience the programme was attempting to stir were watching a quiz show on the other channel – not that Barlow would have been watching that either. Normally, at this time, he would have been having a drink in the pub around the corner. It wasn't a particularly good pub but it was patronised by the less respectable traders of the Vauxhall Bridge Road and the conversation occasionally touched on such matters as stock scheduled to fall off the backs of lorries. Barlow was no longer directly involved in such tiddler-sized crime, but he liked to keep in touch. Having been forcibly extracted from his job as head of CID at Thamesford to become 'Something in the Home Office', he still insisted that he was a policeman and not a superior civil servant digging into nothing deeper than an in-tray. A dog barked sharply on the screen and

Barlow realised with a start that although he had been watching, his brain hadn't absorbed anything that television had been offering for the last five minutes. He forced himself to concentrate and wondered whether the girl was going to put in an appearance again, and if so when.

Barlow remembered her voice from the opening sequence: light, pleasant, slightly upper-middle class but with no corncrake quality. But he preferred faces, so he sat back and waited patiently. The programme was working its way steadily through a succession of interviews with people who were complaining about their local council. The trouble was they looked – and sounded – exactly the same as the people who had been complaining about their local hospital the week before and the same as the ones complaining about their local gas board the week before that. Still, Fenton had asked Barlow to watch this programme and Fenton never did anything without a reason.

Anthony Gordon Fenton, Assistant Secretary, had appeared at Barlow's office with his usual air of being in possession of information calculated to shake everyone else out of their complacency but of being far too considerate to reveal it.

'Ah, Barlow. Glad to have caught you.'

Barlow glanced at the clock.

'There's another three minutes before the bell goes.'

Fenton reflected, as he did virtually every week, that talking to Barlow was like trying to pick up a hedgehog. His polite smile, however, stayed at precisely the right width.

'I wondered whether you had any social engagements this evening.'

Barlow's heart sank. Three months ago, not long after his arrival at the Home Office, Fenton had taken him to dinner at his club. The food had been average, the members middle-aged misfits with nowhere to go and nothing to talk about except the days of old when they had still hoped to be successful. But there was a superb billiards table. Deciding to salvage something from the evening Barlow had suggested that they played for a fiver a game.

Fenton had agreed only with reluctance and Barlow had reached for his cue like a matador going out against a rather small anaemic bull. Fenton had beaten him.

So now Barlow answered warily.

'Nothing of much importance.'

'Then I wonder if I might impose on your leisure hours? There is a television programme due to be transmitted at nine fifteen. One of these current affairs programmes, as I believe they are called. It is concerned with some controversy over a council planning decision somewhere in the North.'

Fenton caught the expression on Barlow's face – or rather the lack of it.

'Quite. Still I suppose it is desirable from time to time to inspect the grass roots of democracy. If it's any consolation I am told the programme is presented by a young lady and, I gather, a rather attractive one. Anyway, I should be grateful if you could find the time to look in. Perhaps we might meet in my office tomorrow morning around ten?'

Barlow nearly opened his mouth to ask why the misdeeds of any local council could possibly interest Fenton but the 'Good night' had been too final: time, tide and the 6.23 to Oxshott waited for no man. For a second Barlow wondered whether to try and catch him up. It would have been tempting to point out that Detective Chief Superintendents weren't television critics and that if any investigation was required he would prefer to do it in person, on the spot, and not through a haze of television speculation. Then the bizarre thought struck him that perhaps Fenton was trying to find him a new interest, or even a new wife. That brought a quick grin to his face, so he settled his bad temper into a shrug. But as he left the office he just thought fleetingly of Fenton on the way to Waterloo and wondered whether he would be watching the programme as well.

But Fenton hadn't gone to Waterloo. Instead, after leaving Barlow he had gone back to his own office. His secretary was collecting her coat and hand-bag and she paused inquiringly as Fenton reappeared. With a wave of the hand he sent her on her way. Waiting until the door had closed behind her he went quietly across to his desk. There were three phones on it: two conventional Post Office instruments with exchange number and extensions on the dial. The third had no markings at all. It was that one Fenton picked up. He waited a few seconds, then gave an extension number. After another brief pause a voice answered. Although, in fact, he had not moved a muscle, anyone watching Fenton would have got the distinct impression that he was standing to attention. But his voice was brisk and matter-of-fact.

'I thought I would just let you know, sir, that I've set the ball rolling.'

The voice at the other end asked a question.

'Yes, sir, he is. A very good man indeed. The best we have.'

The voice quacked again.

'Yes, sir, you can be sure of that. Very carefully indeed. He doesn't even know himself yet. . . . Goodnight.'

Fenton put the phone down and stared at it for a few moments before looking at his watch. It would have to be the 6.37 instead.

The police siren woke Barlow up. He felt the car pulling away and accelerating with a roar, and he reached out his hand for the microphone that should have been on the dashboard in front of him. Instead, the hand hit his glass of whisky from the arm of the chair. He woke with a jolt and remembered where he was. The television set flickered at him. On the screen was a close-up shot of a girl. Barlow had no idea how long he had been asleep or how long she had been there. He concentrated quickly. The programme might be rubbish but the girl was worth looking at.

She was blonde, had a small slightly turned-up nose, hair falling straight to her shoulders and with a spiky fringe. That part of her was dolly bird. The rest wasn't. The eyes were brown and very direct, and her mouth and jaw were strong. The contrast was odd and a trifle disconcerting. The impression was that she might curl up in your lap and then deliver a karate chop once she was comfortable.

Barlow stopped looking and started listening instead. She was introducing the person she was about to interview: the chairman of the local council planning committee who was this week's candidate for interrogation. Barlow began to pay careful attention; this could be it.

The councillor sat squarely in his chair as the questions began. Although he had not been paying attention, Barlow soon picked up the broad outline of the case. Land originally scheduled for housing had now been given by the council to a private developer, the bulk of whose plans consisted of building a hotel, two supermarkets and a bingo hall. The questions were predictable: 'Surely homes should come first. . . ?' So were the answers: 'Ah yes, but you must take a broad view . . .' 'But people are more important. . . ?' '. . . obligation to be fair to all our rate-payers. . . .' The phrases rolled on, and as he listened Barlow grew more and more puzzled. There was something wrong. He leant forward, listening harder, concentrating not so much on the words as on the tone. This wasn't what he had expected at all: the man was honest.

Barlow leant even further towards the screen. This time the camera was on the girl. She too was leaning forward and the strong chin was more prominent. Barlow waited for the question.

'You don't feel, councillor, that your actions – and your motives – could be open to misinterpretation?'

Barlow snorted. What sort of a question was that? Sounding hard but in reality as soft as a feather duster? He stoppered his indignation as the answer came.

'My dear lady' – there was a quick shot of the girl, a small frown starting. Strong on women's lib, thought Barlow, and whoever's directing the cameras knows it. 'If what you are hinting at is that my colleagues and I have been influenced in our decision by anything other than the good of the community as a whole, then I assure you you are quite wrong. We considered the matter, as I have said, very carefully. We knew the decision would be unpopular in some quarters. Nevertheless, I can only repeat, we felt it to be the correct one.'

The voice droned on, one cliché falling onto another. Barlow got up and poured himself another Scotch. This was all wrong. Councillors who had taken graft didn't talk like this. A man with something to hide would have either become very indignant at the merest hint of corruption or blandly ignored it unless ... Barlow concentrated on the screen again.... No. This man wasn't that clever. He was doing himself harm certainly, as it became increasingly evident that, as far as he was concerned, the solid middle-class citizens of the town were the only ones who mattered. But there was nothing further – no sealed envelopes left in overcoat pockets this time.

So why had Fenton asked him to watch? Barlow pondered, decided that he hadn't the faintest idea – and then: unless, that is.... He paused in the act of adding soda to his drink. Then he carried on, but as he lifted the glass to his lips, a very close observer would have noticed that the official face bore the faint trace of a smile.

2

On the stroke of ten Barlow pushed open the door of Fenton's outer office and said a polite good morning to his secretary. The lady in question paused briefly in her typing and smiled acknowledgement. The smile was fairly mechanical. As far as Barlow had been able to establish, the only thing that stirred emotion in Miss Carter's virtually non-existent bosom was the extremely nasty rubber plant that sat beside her desk. Fenton had apparently given it to her one Christmas. Barlow suspected that someone else had given it to Fenton.

'Is his nibs in yet?' he said.

A faint flicker of distaste crossed Miss Carter's face.

'Mr Fenton is expecting you,' she said repressively.

Barlow nodded at the rubber plant.

'That's looking very healthy.'

Contradictory emotions struggled visibly within Miss Carter. No man who liked rubber plants could be all bad. Barlow, enormously cheered by the exchange, opened Fenton's door. As he did so a thought struck him: if he could derive such enjoyment from confusing Miss Carter, then he must be getting very bored indeed. Before he could follow up the thought he was through the door and Fenton was advancing smoothly across the carpet.

'Good morning, Barlow. I trust you spent an enlightening evening.'

'If you mean that load of rubbish you asked me to watch then the answer's no.'

'You didn't feel that the exercise was serving a useful purpose? The value of eternal vigilance. . . ?'

'You may have been eternally vigilant. I fell asleep.'

Fenton's eyes narrowed for a second.

'Dear me, I trust you didn't miss the rest of the programme?'

'I woke up again.'

'I'm glad. I thought it became quite interesting towards the end. I agree the topic wasn't perhaps calculated to rivet the attention, but then it never does to neglect the humdrum daily issues, does it?'

Barlow was getting bored with playing pat-ball. He pulled his chair forward a couple of inches.

'What's she done? Been cheeky to the Foreign Secretary or tried to take the PM's trousers off?'

Fenton did not betray by a flicker how much the abrupt question had disconcerted him. His hands straightened a pile of papers that appeared to be perfectly straight already.

'My dear fellow, when I first met you I was impressed by your shrewdness. I have never felt the need to amend that judgement. You are, as usual, correct. We are concerned with the lady and not with the rather tedious circumstances in which you saw her last night. That merely seemed to me a good opportunity for one-way observation . . . Would you like some tea?'

'No, thank you. I asked a question.'

'You're sure? . . . Yes, I know you did, I don't really think I can give you an answer.'

'You mean you don't know whether she tried to take the PM's trousers off?'

'If she had, that would hardly be a matter for this department. No. But what I would like you to do, if you would be so kind, is to have a word with the lady's husband.'

'Her husband?'

'Yes. He seems to be a trifle worried about her.'

'If I was married to that I'd be worried too.' Barlow pushed back his chair. 'But I'm a policeman, not a marriage guidance councillor.'

Fenton went on, appearing not to notice the interruption.

'I've arranged an appointment for you.' He pushed a slip of paper across the desk. 'You'll find him over at the Foreign Office. Quite a clever young man, I gather. Very highly thought of. He's something of an authority on the livelier parts of the Middle East.' Fenton paused. 'He also bears rather an illustrious name.'

Barlow looked at the paper. He didn't pick it up.

'And he's worried about his wife?'

'Yes. Your appointment's at 10.30. That should give you time. It's not far. And now, if you'll excuse me, I must get my papers together. I'm due at a meeting myself and I need to clear the decks first.'

Barlow got up and moved heavily towards the door. He paused before closing it behind him, dropping the words half over his shoulder.

'Oh, just one thing.'

Fenton looked up.

'When I call to see this young man: Chief Superintendent or Mister?'

'Oh I think "Mister", don't you? After all, he may have nothing to worry about.'

Barlow looked round at Fenton. But Fenton was already bent over his papers.

Back in his own office, Barlow sat for a moment staring at the wall. Then he picked up his phone and buzzed. His secretary answered.

'Get me the Foreign Office, will you?'

He gave her the name he wanted and waited. He was put through very quickly.

'Good morning. My name is Barlow. We had an appointment

this morning. As you're probably aware I didn't make it personally. My feeling is it might be better if we met on neutral ground – and out of office hours.'

He listened to the voice at the other end. It was slightly nervous, a bit disconcerted, with possibly a touch of relief, not just at the change of plan but at the fact that the meeting was postponed. It was a voice that sounded as if it was usually very sure of itself but on this occasion was not. Barlow cut in briskly.

'What part of London do you live?'

The voice told him Campden Hill.

'There's a pub at the top of the hill. Are you well known there? . . . No? . . . Good. I suggest we meet there. Seven thirty? Right. Until then.'

He put the phone down firmly and then went into his outer office. His secretary looked up in surprise as he hauled himself into his coat.

'I'm going out for a couple of hours.'

'What shall I say if anyone asks for you?'

'Tell them I'm out. But if Mr Fenton rings, tell him I've gone to do some research – on contemporary marriage problems.'

The pub was not a good place to arrange to meet anyone. It had three small bars – two of them opening out onto the street. As a result people tended to wait patiently for each other on either side of a panelled partition; the alternative was to shuttle continually in and out of both doors like a figure in a Swiss weather clock. Barlow had chosen it deliberately. He arrived early to make sure that the strategic position he wanted was vacant: it was, so he tucked himself into a corner of the third and smallest bar. From there, half hidden by a serving hatch, one could see the length of both main bars without being seen oneself. Patiently he propped himself against the wall to wait while he went over once again the information he had collected that morning.

It had not amounted to a great deal, but what there was had been intriguing. The world that contained 'respectable' journalism and television 'current affairs' provided more gossip per square inch than practically any other – if you knew where to find it. Barlow had known where to go and that was not to the tavern in Fleet Street with the famous name and the reputation for being the birthplace of the best anecdotes. Instead he put in an appearance at a far less well-known establishment a few hundred yards away in the Strand.

The man he wanted was sitting with a group but detached himself as soon as he saw Barlow come in. He wandered across to him.

'Good morning. Not often we see you in here. What can I get you?' He lowered his voice, 'Business or pleasure?'

'That's very kind of you. I'll have a Scotch . . . a bit of both. Anyone in that lot have anything to do with the county council programme last night?'

'The chap in the corner works on the programme. But I don't think he worked on that particular edition. Would you like the conversation moved that way?'

'Yes please.'

'All right. In exchange you can tell us what the Home Secretary had for breakfast.' Barlow joined the group and was introduced as plain Barlow 'from the Home Office'. At first the group was wary of him but as soon as the conversation moved onto the chosen ground they relaxed, imagining they knew why he was there. In the intervals of acquiring a vast amount of speculation, most of it extraordinarily short on facts, about the alleged misdeeds of local government in the north of England, Barlow managed to slip in a question about the girl.

It had been her colleague on the programme who answered. Phrases from his thumbnail portrait floated into Barlow's mind as he waited:

'Doesn't mix much . . . doesn't try and get any mileage out of being daddy's daughter-in-law either . . . very tough . . . not one of your bra-burning women's libbers but expects to be treated as an equal.' It was one of the others who had asked the inevitable question . . . 'I don't think so. Various chaps have had a go but I don't think anyone's ever got anywhere . . . though there's a rumour she's having a small thing with one of the cameramen. She seems to make sure she always works with him and somebody in the bar the other day was making some crack about the two of them going off to do extra shooting together.' There were masculine guffaws. Barlow waited for a moment.

'What about the husband?'

Information regarding him was less easily obtainable. The consensus seemed to be that professionally at least the two led separate lives. One of the journalists offered a few scraps, largely on the basis of having attended the same university several years earlier . . . 'Looks a bit like a chinless wonder but he isn't . . . He's got his old man's brains but I don't think he's quite as tough . . . Got a slight stammer. I suppose that's why he's in the FO and not working his way up from the back benches.'

None of this had amounted to much. Certainly there had been no hint of anything that could conceivably justify Fenton's interest.

Barlow stopped brooding as the barmaid headed nearer. He started to push his glass towards her, but she stopped and turned to serve a man who had just come into the main bar.

'W-Whisky please.'

So this was the husband who worried about his wife. Barlow leant forward a couple of inches: tallish, just below the six-foot mark, dark hair worn fairly short, narrow horn-rimmed glasses, a sober suit and a rolled umbrella – a penguin from Whitehall, indistinguishable from hundreds of others. Barlow sighed heavily, feeling a wave of nostalgia for the world of straightforward criminals he seemed to have left behind forever. This penguin was nervous though. One hand was twirling his glass round and round with short, jerky movements. Barlow eased himself off his stool. 'Get on with it,' he told himself, 'Chief Superintendent Barlow – hand-holder to the privileged.' The lad didn't even look much like his eminent father.

Viewed across a table, however, the resemblance was more marked. Barlow sat in silence for a moment. Then:

'I gather you're worried about your wife?'

'W-Well, I'm not sure that worried is quite the right word.'

Barlow sighed. This was going to be even more tedious than he had thought.

'Let's try another word. Concerned, for example. Worried, concerned, troubled. Let's not bother too much at this stage about the degree of emotion. I'm more interested in the way it affects you.'

'How do you mean?'

'Well, put it this way. A man is worried about his wife. I beg your pardon. He's concerned about his wife. Now there are various people he might go and talk to about it. A doctor; a psychiatrist even: a social worker or a priest. But you didn't. You asked to see a policeman.'

'I d-didn't ask to see you.'

'Not in so many words, perhaps. But you pushed buttons. And you must have known that if you pushed those particular buttons, then someone like me would turn up at the other end.'

'L-look, Chief Superintendent, I should explain. I d-didn't – as you put it – push any buttons at all. In fact, I can only apologise for having dragged you out here like this. P-perhaps I might buy you a drink to compensate for your trouble?'

'I'll have a whisky. A large one.'

Barlow waited until the drink was put before him.

'So you didn't push buttons. Somebody did. And not many people know where they keep those particular buttons. If it wasn't you, it must have been your father. So why is he worried about your wife?'

'M-my father is worried about a great many things.'

'Yes, I know. That's what he's paid for. I'm paid, some of the time, to worry about things that are worrying him. At the moment, I'm not earning my money. I know. We'll make a game out of it. I'll start guessing and you say "Warm" or "Cold".

Right. Men. She's having an affair and you're afraid of the scandal.'

'Of course not. You're being unnecessarily offensive.'

'I'm just trying to get somewhere. Drugs. She's on mainline.'

'D-don't be ridiculous . . . I'm s-sorry. I appreciate that you're only acting in response to a request from your superiors but I really feel that there is nothing to be gained by continuing this conversation.'

'Well, at least I know why you're worried about your wife. So I've got something out of it.'

He had half risen but as Barlow spoke, he lowered himself back into his seat.

'What do you mean? How can you know?'

'It's money. It has to be. Sex, drugs, money. There isn't anything else. Unless she's selling secrets to the Russians. And if it was that, you wouldn't be talking to me.'

The two men looked at each other. Barlow totally placid and calm, his companion tense and uneasy. Suddenly he removed his glasses and rubbed his eyes. The gesture made him look much younger and more vulnerable beneath the official disguise. Barlow got up.

'Listen, lad. You're an up-and-coming civil servant at one end of Whitehall. I'm a fairly up-and-come one at the other end. I'm also twenty years older than you and I've spent half my life listening to people and keeping my mouth shut afterwards. I'll buy you a Scotch, you tell me what's bothering you and I'll tell you if I can do anything about it. Then we'll both go home.'

When he got back from the bar, the spectacles were back on but the effect was less pompous and severe. This time as he started to talk, Barlow noticed that the stammer disappeared.

'I'm sorry. It's still going to be a waste of your time, I'm afraid. It's just that . . . well, my father does have a tendency to overreact to things. But it's just that . . . well . . . You were right. It is money. It's not so much worrying as puzzling. Except that I can't think of any explanation which is not a worry in itself.'

Barlow pushed the other whisky across the table.

'If that's the way you write minutes in the Foreign Office, it's no wonder this country is in the state it's in.'

He got a grin in return.

'I'm sorry. I seem to have said that several times in the last couple of minutes. In fact the problem is very simple. A couple of weeks ago I saw my wife's bank statement. We have separate accounts. She works and she does what she likes with her money. I don't mean she only spends it on herself. She buys things for the house and so on. But it's her own money. I don't know how healthy her account is unless she tells me.'

'And does she?'

'Oh yes. We both know roughly how much money we have between us at any given moment.'

'But this time you saw her bank statement?'

'Yes. By accident. It was on her desk, I was looking for a telephone number in the book and . . .'

'She was heavily overdrawn all of a sudden?'

'Oh no. She had just about what she should have had.'

'So what's the problem? If it was my wife I'd be relieved not worried.'

'Yes, but there was one very odd thing. Her pay cheques were credited. But there were other credits as well. Quite large ones. They averaged about £200 a month.'

'Does your wife do any other work? Writing articles for instance.'

'She does occasionally but I know about those.'

'Wait a minute. If these sums of money are being paid in, why hasn't she got more money than you would expect?'

'That's the point. According to her bank statement, she's paying them straight back out again. Exactly the same amount every month. It arrives from somewhere – and it goes somewhere. The bank statement went back to the beginning of the year. The same thing happened every month.'

Barlow thought for a moment. He would have to tread carefully.

'I can see it's odd, worrying even. It's not the kind of thing you can ask about either.' He paused. 'Or did you have a go?'

Once again, he got the grin, but a trifle rueful this time.

'Yes, I did.'

'What happened?'

'We had a row. A very noisy one. My wife made most of the noise. It didn't amount to much except that she said it was none of my business.'

'And that was that?'

'Yes. Except that I got the impression she wasn't so much angry that I'd been snooping. I wouldn't have minded that.'

'What then? What impression did you get?'

'Frightened. I got the impression she was scared stiff.'

3

'Can you fix it? . . . As soon as possible really . . . Yes, that would do. It sounds as good an excuse as any. I don't want to be tied down though, so make it informal. I want to be able to get anywhere I want to . . . OK. Ring me back.'

Barlow put the phone down. It was the morning after his conversation in the pub. Simon – they had eventually got on Christian-name terms – had added nothing more that was of any use to Barlow. But he had obviously wanted to talk, so Barlow had let him. Just before leaving he said again:

'What worries me is just that I can't think of any explanation that makes sense.'

Barlow refrained from telling him that he could think of at least five.

The next stage was to talk to the lady in the case. Except, of course, that there wasn't a case. Not yet anyway. Still, it would be interesting to meet her – in the flesh.

It took two days for the call he was waiting for to come through.

'Well, I've got you in,' said the voice from the office on the floor below his. 'They were a bit baffled. Normally these things are arranged by committees. But they couldn't very well turn us down flat. They said you should go to the studios in Shepherd's

Bush. That's where the current affairs programmes are produced. The head of the department is a man called Henderson. He's expecting you tomorrow, 9.30. I hope you get what you want.'

'So do I,' said Barlow. 'The trouble is I haven't even got to the stage of knowing what I want. But thank you for your help.'

'Not at all. You've got the details? Henderson, Shepherd's Bush, 9.30.'

Barlow was there at 9.15 because he always liked to arrive early. It gave him a chance to see what was going on before other people started showing him. The receptionist proved amiable, directing him to the canteen and offering to have him paged as soon as Mr Henderson arrived.

Barlow sipped his coffee and listened to the groups at the tables near him. It was desultory, early-morning conversation much the same in tone as that at a police canteen: one or two jokes about hangovers, a certain amount of grumbling at having to start work again. There was even some discussion of last night's television programmes – praise, blame, occasional mockery. Only one thing made it different. Members of the public would have been talking about the performers, the actors. These groups instead mentioned directors, producers, cameramen. Their assessments were professional.

As he sat and listened, Barlow was conscious that an occasional glance was being thrown his way. Presumably strangers were a rarity in the canteen at this hour of the morning, so it was understandable that they should wonder what he was doing there.

Come to that he was wondering himself. He had been tempted to go and see Fenton, give him what information he had and suggest politely but firmly that the whole matter could be disposed of by referring young Simon and his father to a reliable firm of private detectives. He had been tempted but he hadn't done so. He wasn't even sure why, except that he had rather liked the worried husband. It was just then that the wife came through the doors of the canteen.

A number of heads half turned and a fair number of male eyes stayed watching her as she went up to the counter. Even at that hour of the morning, thought Barlow, she was worth looking at. The man who had come in with her paused, looked around the canteen and came towards Barlow.

'Good morning. I'm John Henderson. You're Mr Barlow. Would you like another coffee?'

Barlow hesitated.

'Yes, you would. Maggie!' He called over his shoulder and the girl turned her head. 'Make it three!'

He sat down, giving Barlow an amiable smile.

'I gather you want to come and wander around for a bit just to see what happens. My bosses said something about a report?'

'Yes, that's right. The police are getting a bit more used to the idea of chaps like you looking over their shoulder all the time. I don't suppose we'll ever get to like it but we might get used to it. Anyway, I've been asked to look into the whole area of liaison between the television organisations and the police and I thought that it would be a good idea if I found out how people like you work.'

'Thank you, love.'

Barlow blinked and then realised that the remark was addressed to the girl who was standing beside him with the coffee.

'Maggie, this is Mr Barlow; Maggie Everrett. Maggie's a reporter. Mr Barlow's a policeman.'

'Really. How interesting.'

Her tone of voice implied that it was actually nothing of the kind.

'Do you take sugar?'

'No thank you. Bad for my weight.'

Her eyes flicked deliberately towards his waistline and then away. This time she made no comment at all. Barlow controlled a sense of irritation. He wasn't used to such total indifference. In fact, it was almost too pointed, and, although he might have been imagining it, he thought he had caught a slight underlining, almost a warning note, in Henderson's brisk introduction of him and his job virtually in the same breath.

Henderson was talking again:

'I think the best thing I can do is to take you along to meet the editor of our twice-weekly programme and suggest to him that you just sit in on the day as it goes along. I am afraid you may find it a bit confusing but that seems more sensible than giving you a formal guide. Apart from anything else,' he smiled disarmingly, 'I haven't got anyone free for the job.'

'That would suit me fine,' said Barlow. 'You work on that programme, Miss Everrett?'

'Yes.'

He waited but she left it at that.

'If you had a moment to spare perhaps you could help me with anything I find too confusing.'

'I'm afraid I shall be dodging about today. I've a lot of filming to organise.'

'What is your film about?'

'Oh it's not very interesting. And nothing may come of it, anyway. Now, if you'll excuse me, I must go and find the crew.'

She got up, nodded to Henderson and left with, once again, a steady searchlight beam of male eyes following her. Barlow looked at Henderson.

'Friendly little thing.'

'Maggie?' Henderson was obviously a little embarrassed. 'Yes, I'm sorry, she was a bit brusque. She gets very wrapped up in her work. I expect she's just preoccupied – as I have to become. We'll move if you don't mind.'

Barlow followed Henderson out of the canteen and along a passageway. At the end, Henderson stopped before a heavy, sound-proofed door.

'Here you are,' he said. 'Welcome to the dream factory.'

As he pushed the door open and walked in, Barlow saw that they were in a large studio which appeared to be used as a store-room. It reminded him of some giant children's playroom. Huge toy building blocks were littered about and bits and pieces of scenery and equipment that he recognised – a large globe that he had occasionally seen hovering in editions of 'Panorama' leant drunkenly up against a board with last Saturday's racing results on it. In the corner a relief map of Africa was propped up against a model farm. Henderson caught his surprise and wonder about the farm.

'We share a studio with a children's programme,' he said and marched him past a six-foot high blow-up of the Milky Way that Barlow remembered seeing Patrick Moore waving his eyebrows at. Next to it a blow-up of Edward Heath and another of Lloyd George were having an eye-ball to eye-ball confrontation. Lloyd George appeared to be winning.

'Have you ever been in a studio gallery?' Henderson asked as they turned a corner and headed towards a lift.

'No,' said Barlow.

'In that case you could watch from there this evening. There's nothing happening at the moment, so we'll go up to the production offices. I'll just ring through and see that everything's all right.'

'Is there any reason why it shouldn't be?'

But Henderson had already moved to an internal phone alongside the lift. He didn't hear the question or, possibly, had chosen not to. Barlow listened as he dialled a number.

'It's John Henderson here. I have Mr Barlow with me and I was just going to bring him along to the office. OK? . . . Fine. We'll come up.'

In silence they stood in the lift which, like the rest of the building, was old and shabby, badly in need of paint. After such dinginess and the jumble-sale air of the scenery dock through which they had passed, the production offices themselves took Barlow by surprise. He blinked as the doors opened. The long, low room looked rather like the control centre for a space launch. Television monitors were ranged down the centre and there appeared to be several hundred telephones. White boards hung on the walls with letters, numbers and code-names printed on them. There was a low murmur of talk and the occasional clatter of a typewriter. As Barlow recovered, however, he realised that the initial austere, impersonal impression was deceptive.

Scattered over every surface was an untidy clutter of crumpled newspapers, limp cardboard coffee cups and scraps of paper with random scribbling all over them. In fact, the only objects which didn't contain papers were the wire trays which were presumably intended to. They were all empty except for two which had been placed one on top of the other to form a small cage. Inside it was a hamster.

The hamster apart, it could, thought Barlow, have been the operations room at Thamesford – but there were two major differences. It was infinitely untidier and the people were not in uniform. On the contrary, they seemed to be dressed in a kind of anti-uniform. One or two of the men wore suits, others were in sweaters and jeans. One wore a shirt and a pair of pink trousers. All the girls were wearing trousers except one who wore a short skirt. Barlow noticed her extremely good legs which presumably accounted for the distinction.

Henderson led him over to a desk behind which a girl was talking urgently into a telephone. As she saw them approaching she put it down, as far as Barlow could tell without letting the person at the other end know she was about to do so.

'Good morning, Jill,' said Henderson. 'This is Mr Barlow. Did Tom tell you all about him?' The girl nodded and, once again, Barlow got a faint sense of a message being transmitted and understood.

'I'll leave you with Jill then,' said Henderson. 'She knows more about what's going on than anybody else, certainly more than I do. But we might meet for a drink later? Jill will bring you down to my office.'

He waved a hand vaguely and wandered away. Barlow was left looking at the girl. She was small and blonde, with an air of brisk determination. She made Barlow feel old. As he inspected her, she half turned in her chair and shouted towards a bank of filing cabinets behind her.

'Sue? Can we have two coffees?'

'Piss off,' said a cheerful female voice from behind the cabinets.

'It's for a visitor.'

'Coming up,' said the voice equally cheerfully.

Barlow decided that perhaps it was even less like the operations room at Thamesford than he had first thought. From behind the cabinet rose a plume of steam – presumably the first stages of his coffee.

'What do you do?' he asked Jill. 'Apart from getting stuck with people like me.'

If he had been hoping for a polite denial that she was stuck with him, he didn't get it. Instead, Jill swung her chair around to face one of the boards behind her.

'I'm called the co-ordinator,' she said. 'Any plans for stories that we're going to film or items arranged in advance come to me. I write them on that board and generally keep tabs on everything . . . what the reporters are doing and so on.'

'How many reporters are there?'

'Five. Four men and one girl.'

'That's Maggie. I met her in the canteen this morning.'

'That's right,' said Liz.

A hand appeared over the filing cabinet holding a cup of coffee. Jill took it and passed it to Barlow.

'And what are the reporters doing?'

Jill looked at the board, although she gave the impression that she hardly needed to use it, and began to recite in a rapid monotone: 'There's Tom Grainger, he's in Kenya, due back at the end of this week. There's a crew in France and a reporter and director are going out to join up with them tomorrow. They've been filming for another programme – the crew have, I mean. Andy Sullivan is the reporter and the director is Brian Phillips. Then there's one reporter in Leeds on an industrial story and another down in Dover doing the 495th story about the Channel Tunnel.'

'If there have been all that many stories, why do another one?'

'Well, there aren't all that many new stories. Besides,' she said with a grin, 'it is one of those stories that people never get tired of – like comprehensive schools and bring back British Summer Time.' She settled down to elaborate on her theme but Barlow cut in.

'What's the Welsh story?'

'Pardon?'

'The Welsh story. It's on the board behind you. It says "Welsh story. Travel 29th. Film 30th." It's the 29th today.'

'Oh, that's been postponed. In fact, I think it may even be cancelled. I must check and rub it off.'

Barlow got up, leaned over and put his cup down on the desk in front of her.

'That was very good,' he said. 'The coffee, I mean. And I enjoyed our chat very much. Very interesting – and quite clever too. Tell your boss from me that I thought you did very well.'

He turned away and strolled down the office, leaving Jill looking after him with a slightly wary expression. The girl who had made the coffee popped her head over the nearest filing cabinet.

'How's the policeman? He looks a bit stodgy. Is he boring?'

'I don't think so,' said Jill thoughtfully looking at Barlow's retreating back. 'I think he's rather bright. In fact, I think he's a bit brighter than we thought he was going to be.'

Barlow continued his saunter down the length of the office and turned along a corridor. It was the way he had seen Henderson disappearing, and as he reached the end of the corridor, he heard voices. Barlow stopped to listen. They appeared to be coming from the door on his left. Henderson was talking. Then the girl, Maggie, answered him. Barlow moved closer.

'Look, love, don't worry.' Henderson was speaking. 'I don't know for sure why he's here any more than you do. It could be a cover story; on the other hand, it could be just coincidence. Either way, there's no point in getting all steamed up about it. Just carry on as if nothing had happened. But be a bit careful, that's all.'

'That's all right for you. If there is trouble you can just wash your hands of it. I'm the one who'll get stuck with the police.'

Barlow heard the sound of a door handle being turned and spun smartly on his heel. He went back to Jill's desk and pulled up a chair.

'There's one thing I forgot to get clear,' he said.

'What was that?'

'When you gave me that list of what the reporters were doing. I assume that they don't always come back to base after every story, do they?'

'Oh God, no. That would just be a waste of time. No, we try and arrange a number of stories fairly near each other so that they can move on from one to the next. The fellow in Leeds, for example . . . when he's finished there he goes on to Manchester.'

'I thought that's how it would work. And the man doing the Channel Tunnel story will go on to France?'

'That's right.'

So far Jill had been half talking and half watching one of the television monitor screens which showed a studio rehearsal in progress. Suddenly Barlow saw he had her full attention. She opened her mouth as if to say more, then shut it again.

'Well, I mustn't hold you up,' said Barlow. 'You'd better go on with your checking.'

'Checking?'

'Yes. The Welsh story, don't you remember? You haven't rubbed it off the board yet.'

Jill hesitated for a second.

'I can't yet. The researcher in charge of it won't be available until lunch-time.'

'Well, well,' said Barlow. He was beginning to enjoy himself. 'That means we're both stuck for what to do next, aren't we?'

'No we aren't.' Jill got up with an air of brisk determination. 'I'll take you on a tour and explain everything to you. Come on. We'll start with the teleprinter service – where the news comes in.'

Two hours later it was only the knowledge that his gauntlet

lightly flipped down had been picked up and slapped back in his face that was keeping Barlow going. He had been subjected to an exhaustive guided tour of every aspect of the production of a television current affairs programme, and Jill had hammered information into him as if she were a riveter working at a triple bonus rate. He had seen the news tapes chattering off the Reuter and the Press Association teleprinters, the library of press cuttings on every conceivable subject, the photographic dark-room where still pictures were processed and the graphics room where animated captions were prepared. He had been towed remorselessly through the film editors' rooms where film was coiling about like spaghetti and men talked a strange jargon of 'creeping sync' and 'inter-neg' and chatted about 'cut-aways' and 'Noddies'. 'Cut-aways' he discovered were interviewers' questions filmed after the interview had been completed but at a different angle so they could be inserted into the main interview itself. 'Noddies' were a similar exercise but consisted of dumb nods of assent, scratchings of the left ear and similar mimed gestures to show the interviewer paying attention as his subject answered.

From the so-called 'cutting rooms' he had been taken into the studio gallery and the lighting console had been explained at interminable length. His comprehension of that had not been helped by Jill having introduced a tall, gloomy man as 'This is Bill, he's the Tom,' until it had then been explained that 'Tom' stood for Technical Operations Manager – the engineer in charge of the working of the studio. Through the whole tour, however, Barlow kept expecting to see the girl, Maggie. Surely she should be somewhere along the production line either in the offices or in the film section. But it was possible that she had left the building, in which case he was wasting his time. More likely, of course, he was having his time wasted for him. Whichever was the case, Barlow decided to call a halt.

'Does this place have a bar?'

'Yes,' said Jill. 'The club is just off the yard where the film offices are. We'll be able to stop there and I'll show you how a camera works.'

'I know how a camera works,' said Barlow taking her by the elbow. 'Why don't I buy you a drink and you can tell me all about the people who work here? After all, I'm a policeman, remember, and policemen are always interested in people.'

As he stood aside to let Jill go ahead of him, he caught her expression and decided that, at least, the scores were now level again.

4

The 'club' turned out to be a large room with a bar at one end and a sandwich counter at the other. It was full of people – all of them, it seemed to Barlow, talking and hardly any of them listening. He collected his whisky and the Campari and soda that Jill had ordered and pushed his way back across the room to where she was sitting.

'Well,' he said, as he raised his glass to her. 'This is cosy.'

Jill looked startled for a second and then laughed.

'So you have got a sense of humour after all,' she said. Then, abruptly, she leant forward. 'Why are you really here, Mr Barlow?'

Barlow took a sip of his drink.

'Didn't your boss tell you?'

'You mean that stuff about trying to establish better liaison between the police and television? Oh yes, we got all that.'

'But you don't believe it?'

'No. I did until I saw you. But the moment you walked into the room I knew there were . . . that there had to be another reason.'

Barlow ignored the half slip of the tongue.

'Why should you think that just because I walked into the room?'

'You don't look right. We quite often have people coming on

these liaison things. They all look the same and they all sound the same. They're people who aren't any good at doing their own job, so they get pushed off into some kind of PR thing like that.'

'And you don't think I look that sort?'

'I know you aren't. You behave as if you're working – and not at liaison either.'

Barlow leaned back in his chair.

'The trouble with you, my girl, is that you've been in this place too long. You think everything has to be like it is on the tele. Well, it isn't. So instead of chasing mysteries that don't exist, why don't I buy you another drink and we'll talk about something else?'

Three hours later Barlow was beginning to get annoyed. As a policeman he was used to people being obstructive, lying to him, or just refusing to say anything at all. But he had never before come across such cheerful co-operation which, at the same time, was managing to conceal the one piece of information he wanted. He was now totally familiar with the immediate plans of every member of the programme – except those of Maggie Everrett. He had attended the afternoon viewing of films and listened while the plans for that evening's programmes were finalised. Jill had gossipped happily about the programme itself and the personalities involved in it. Whatever questions he had asked had been readily answered but not one scrap of information had been volunteered. All he had to go on were the half-rubbed-out words on the board behind her desk.

It was then that he had his stroke of luck. Jill had disappeared for a moment, leaving him alone, when her phone rang. Barlow automatically picked it up.

'Is Jill there,' said a man's voice.

'No,' said Barlow. 'She'll be back in a moment. Can I give her a message or ask her to call you back?'

'No, it's all right,' said the voice. 'It's Reg Field here. I said I'd ring and tell her where we were booked in. Got a Biro handy?'

'Yes.'

'Right. It's the George Hotel, Pontrhyd. Got that? The phone number is Pontrhyd 382.'

'OK,' said Barlow. 'I'll tell her.'

He put the phone down, looked at his scribbled message, folded the paper and put it carefully into his pocket. Then he got up and strolled across to the opposite corner of the office. In his earlier tour of inspection he had noticed a list of people connected with the programme pinned to the wall there. A quick glance found him the name he was looking for ... 'R. Field – film cameraman'. All he needed now was to remember why the name Pontrhyd sounded so very familiar.

He was still trying to remember as he and Jill walked into the club again. The programme had been recorded. It seemed to have gone reasonably well and there was an air of exuberant relaxation about the group who stood around the bar. Barlow bought drinks and steered Jill towards two chairs. Sitting opposite her he leant forward:

'Now I'm going to ask you a question.'

'Can I have a cigarette first?'

Barlow gave her one, lit it for her and waited until he had her attention again.

'At lunch-time you said you didn't think I was here just on some liaison job. Now. My question. Why should I be here for some other reason?'

'But I told you ... You don't look like ...'

'No, that wasn't what I asked you. Why should you assume, the moment you heard a policeman was appearing on the scene, that he was after something in particular. And not just you ... the others as well.'

'But that's you jumping to conclusions. Just because I thought you didn't look the part, why should you assume I know what you could be after? You could be snooping around for some reason of your own.'

'Your reaction's wrong. And not just yours – everybody's. Behaving as if there was something that had to be kept from me

. . . like a lot of kids with a secret. And that nonsense of yours with the list of reporters. Trying to make four sound like five.'

Barlow stood up.

'Listen to me. I'm off now. But I'll tell you this much. If I were here for any other reason and you were trying to stop me, then that would be silly. Because that would make me angry. And none of you would like that. So pass that on around your grapevine. OK?'

As he left the club he saw Jill moving over to talk to the other members of the production team. She was looking thoughtful. They were still discussing Barlow's parting words an hour later when the doorman called Jill to the phone.

'Jill,' said the caller, 'It's Reg Field here. Sorry to bother you, love, but I can't get a reply from the film office. We need some more film stock.'

'That's all right, Reg,' said Jill. 'I'll look after it. Where do you want it sent?'

'To the hotel.'

'Yes, but which hotel? Where are you staying?'

'Didn't they give you the message?'

'What message?'

'I phoned this afternoon. It's the George Hotel, Pontrhyd.'

'That's Liz,' said Jill. 'She's always taking messages and forgetting to pass them on.'

'No, it wasn't Liz this time. It was some feller. I didn't know his voice. But he wrote it all down. Anyway, not to worry. Just send the stock. See you, love.'

He rang off, leaving Jill staring into the phone. Slowly she pressed the receiver and then dialled a number. She waited while it rang steadily for several minutes and then put the receiver back.

'Nobody there?' said the doorman.

'No,' said Jill. 'Still, I expect it will keep until the morning.'

She was wrong though. As she turned to walk back into the club, Barlow was driving out of London and along the M4 motorway towards the Severn Bridge and South Wales. He was driving fast, and, alerted by a phone call, there was a detective inspector waiting for him at the other end. Chief Superintendent Barlow had remembered why the name Pontrhyd was so familiar.

5

Barlow had decided to stay at Pontrhyd's other main hotel, the Royal. It looked as if a showdown with Miss Maggie Everrett was due fairly soon but he preferred to have it at a moment of his own choosing. Meanwhile he studied the man sitting in the easy chair opposite, the Detective Inspector he had asked for.

'It's been some time since we worked together.'

'It has indeed. I was Detective Sergeant Price then.'

'You were. And I was solving nice simple crimes instead of playing nurse-maid to the rich or famous.'

'Is that what you are doing in Pontrhyd, Mr Barlow? It doesn't sound like you. It doesn't sound like Pontrhyd either, come to that.'

'I'm not sure what I am doing in Pontrhyd. Except that a number of quite bright, intelligent young people seemed to think it was essential that I be kept away.'

Detective Inspector Price knew better than to ask questions. Instead he sipped his drink and waited, while Barlow fell silent, staring at the table between them. Suddenly he looked up.

'Tell me about the Forrester case.'

Price sat up with a jerk.

'What do you want to know about that for?'

He encountered the glare, acknowledged it with a lift of his hand and settled back into his seat again.

'Sorry, sir. You just took me by surprise, that's all, although come to think of it, I should have guessed that was what you were down here about.'

'Why? It's all over and forgotten, isn't it?'

'Well, yes and no, really.'

'Stop talking in riddles.'

'Well . . . the background you know. Forrester was sent down. Three years. The sentence was a bit savage. He'd never been more than a nuisance really. But the evidence was very strong. They found a couple of guns in the house, plans and papers and so on. A do-it-yourself bomb kit. The judge said if he'd stuck to making "Wales for the Welsh" speeches he would have been all right but this was plotting violence and he wasn't having that kind of thing. So down went Forrester.'

'Forrester claimed all the stuff had been planted on him?'

'That's right.'

'And the evidence was all police evidence?'

'Yes. More or less. All the evidence that mattered.' Price was becoming wary. He looked across at Barlow. 'You know all of this anyway. Your people were asked to check on any tie-ups with other organisations in your area.'

'Yes, I know. I was just making sure my memory wasn't playing tricks. There were two officers involved, weren't there? Jones and that sergeant, what was his name?'

'Bill Jenkins. Jones is my boss now. Jenkins is dead.'

'Dead? How?'

'Car accident. He was driving home late one night and he hit a lorry.'

'I see . . . Do you want another drink?'

Price nodded and Barlow picked up their glasses and strolled over to the bar. When he came back he paused before putting them down on the table.

'Forrester made a lot of wild accusations in the dock, didn't he? About it all being a frame up?'

'That's right. I suspect that's why the judge went for him the way he did. Judges don't approve of that sort of thing.'

'Have you ever thought Forrester might have been telling the truth?'

Price let out a long breath and glared at his glass still on the table. He looked at the man opposite him, remembering what he knew of him at first hand and what he had been told. He remembered one of his colleagues saying only half jokingly: 'Barlow? I'd rather have a Dobermann Pinscher after me.' This was not going to be easy. But he had to try.

'Look, Mr Barlow, it's a long time ago. Forrester has got about a month to go before he comes out. So he has done his time. Apart from anything else, he turned into a martyr after the trial whereas he was always regarded as a bit of a fool before. If anything, we did him a favour by getting him put away. Jenkins is dead. Jones is a senior officer. What good will it do to rake it all up again? Why don't we just let it all be forgotten?'

Barlow said nothing for a moment. Then he picked up his glass and drained it.

'It's your turn.'

With a barely concealed sigh of relief Price got to his feet and went over to the bar. He brought the drinks back and settled into his chair again. Barlow waited until he had taken a sip.

'Why are you so sure that those two framed Forrester?'

Price's relaxed air fell off him like a cloak.

'I never said that.'

'Look, Inspector, don't try and play pat-ball with me. There were rumours at the time that there was something odd about that case. And you've been as nervy as a kitten ever since I started talking about it. And you wouldn't suggest that the whole thing was better left alone unless you knew something. So tell me – before I start picking up phones and getting chief constables out of bed.'

Price got up, walked across the lounge and closed the door that led into the bar area. He came back and pulled his chair up to the table.

'Listen, Mr Barlow, I've got no evidence. I've got no proof.

Nothing. If I had, I would have used it as best I could in a case that wasn't mine anyway. You know me well enough to believe that. However much I didn't like Forrester – and I didn't – I wouldn't have just stood back and let him serve three years for nothing.'

'I believe you. But there's something. What is it?'

Price squirmed in his chair, looking even unhappier than before. He had the air of a man who, having undergone the dentist's examination, had just been told that all his teeth would have to go.

'Sir, I didn't think things fitted from the start. Forrester was a great man for making speeches. He was a great one for telling youngsters that they should be prepared to commit acts of violence in the sacred name of Wales. He probably wouldn't have been all that bothered if one of his youngsters had found a gun from somewhere. But he never struck me as the sort of man to have guns himself. I don't think he had the guts apart from anything else.'

'So it smelt wrong. What else?'

Price almost blushed. 'Fervour in Wales, sir – whether in politics or religion – is often accompanied by, well, randiness. Forrester had a reputation for collecting girls, using them, then discarding them. He didn't do it kindly.'

'And one girl . . . ?' Barlow prompted very quietly.

'It was three months before Forrester was arrested. One girl he turned out – and she tried to kill herself. She didn't succeed. It was hushed up and she's living with an aunt up Manchester way . . .'

'So she informed on Forrester?'

'Possibly so. She wouldn't have had far to go.'

'Where?' Barlow was impatient.

'She had – she has – an uncle here. Like a father he was to her, she always said.' Price paused, but Barlow had no need to utter his 'Who?'

'Her uncle was Inspector Jones!'

'More like a father,' echoed Barlow.

Price finished what was left in his glass, put it down and stared at Barlow.

'It's not evidence, Mr Barlow. And it's a while ago now. If Forrester still had a long time to serve I wouldn't be arguing like this. But he's due out any day now. Much better just to leave it alone.'

Barlow pushed back the table and got up. Price did the same and together they walked towards the door. Barlow said nothing as they passed through the hotel lobby until they were alone again in the street outside.

'Who knows you've been talking to me?'

'Well . . . not many people. We just got a request from the Home Office via the Chief Constable, saying you were coming down and asking that I be put at your disposal.'

'All right. I'll be calling on your chief tomorrow morning. Just a courtesy call.'

'And will you still want me tomorrow?'

'I don't know yet. But I can tell you this. Even if I wanted to, I don't think I am going to be able to leave the Forrester case alone. You know there's a television team from London in the town?'

'Yes. They're doing some story about the decline of the mining industry or something.'

'That's what they may have told people. I don't think they are. I think they're doing a story about the Forrester case. And that means we haven't got very much time.'

'Do you want me . . . ?'

'Just get back to the station. Keep mum about this. I'll call you very soon.'

'Right, sir. Here's the number.'

Barlow watched Price drive away, then looked at his watch. It was nearly 10.30. He turned to the hotel porter who was maintaining a fairly listless vigil outside.

'What time is stop-tap around here?'

'Eleven o'clock, sir.'

'Thank you,' said Barlow. He began to walk slowly down the street. The George Hotel was only five minutes away, and when he reached it all three bars were still doing a brisk trade. He stood just outside the entrance to the lounge, watching the girl. She was dressed in trousers and a loose sweater but she somehow still contrived to look smarter than the three other women in the room who had obviously gone to a good deal more trouble. The man with her, Barlow assumed, was the director. He was short and dark, wearing a suede jacket.

The pair were sharing a bottle of wine and appeared to be arguing. As Barlow watched the man took her hand, apparently to hold her attention on something he was saying. He got her attention but he did not let go of her hand.

Barlow turned away and went up to the reception desk. The night porter was reading the evening paper. Barlow paused to give thanks that he was in South Wales. He remembered telling John Watt once that it was the easiest area in Britain in which to obtain information! 'The point is, John, they're so nosey themselves that they think it's peculiar if you don't ask questions . . .'

The porter put away his paper as Barlow approached.

'Good evening, sir. What can I do for you?'

'I'd like to borrow that train time-table if I may?'

'Certainly, sir.'

Barlow flicked through the pages, looking for the main-line service to London.

'I see you've got the tele staying with you.'

'Oh, Miss Everrett, you mean? Yes indeed. Booked in this afternoon they did. There's five of them altogether.'

'I've seen Miss Everrett on the screen. I suppose the man with her is the producer?'

'That would be Mr Downes. The director he calls himself . . . If you are looking for trains to London, the first one is ten past eight.'

'Oh, thank you.' Barlow handed the book back. 'I needn't have bothered, need I? Is there a phone I could use down here?'

'There's the one in the far corner if it's private. Or you can use this one here.'

'Thanks again.'

Barlow moved towards the corner. The porter watched him go like a fisherman who has seen his best fly totally ignored. Barlow dialled and the phone was answered almost immediately.

'Price? . . . It's Barlow. I'm at the George. I want you to do something for me. There's a bloke staying here called Downes. He's the director of that television team. In – let me see – five minutes precisely I want you to ring through here and have him paged. He's in the lounge bar. Tell him who you are and say you want to talk to him privately. Say it's urgent and you must see him straight away. Don't commit yourself to anything specific but get him out of here and keep him out for half an hour . . . What? . . . I don't care what you do with him after that. Half an hour is all I need . . . Oh, tell him you've got cold feet or you need more time to think. But put through that call in exactly five minutes. Got that? Right. I'll phone you tomorrow.'

He turned and walked briskly into the lounge bar. The two of them didn't see him until he was beside their table with his hand already on the back of an empty chair.

'Good evening. What a pleasant surprise! May I join you?'

The man merely looked up in astonishment. The girl, Barlow was pleased to notice, looked extremely annoyed. Before either of them had a chance to say anything, Barlow slid into the chair and signalled to the waiter.

'Would you bring another bottle, please, and a third glass.'

Barlow beamed at the girl.

'Well, aren't you going to introduce us?'

'This is Mr Barlow. He's a policeman – from London. This is John Downes. He works for the same programme as I do.'

'A policeman from London?'

Downes was looking wary and a trifle bemused. Barlow could sympathise with him. The girl continued:

'Yes. I met Mr Barlow in the studios. He was on some sort of liaison visit.'

Downes stopped looking bemused and became extremely wary indeed.

'Oh, you're the . . .'

The girl broke in.

'That's right. Remember? I was telling you I'd met Mr Barlow in the canteen.'

'Yes. I remember. And what brings you to Pontrhyd, Mr Barlow?'

'Oh. Just visiting.'

'Business or pleasure?'

'Business. And you?'

'We're working. We're doing a story on the decline of the mining industry.'

'Yes. So I heard.'

They had both been beginning to relax slightly but now they tensed again.

'Oh? Who told you? The office in London?'

'Oh no. They don't even know I'm here. In fact, they seemed to be under the impression that your story had been scrubbed.'

Barlow noticed the flicker that passed across Downes's face. He was beginning to enjoy himself.

'So who did tell you what we were doing?'

'One of the local people. In fact, I heard all about you almost as soon as I arrived. The man who told me was very worked up about it. Have you come across him? He's the local detective inspector. His name's Price.

'No, I haven't met him.'

'No, of course, you wouldn't', said Barlow blandly. 'You would have been to see Chief Inspector Jones, wouldn't you?' He paused to observe the effect of his words. 'After all, he's the senior officer around here. Did you get what you wanted from him?'

'Yes thank you. He was very helpful.'

Downes had the air of a man who had no idea what kind of bowling he was facing and so had decided to play a straight bat to everything.

'Good. Let me know if he isn't being as co-operative as you think he might be.'

'Why?' The girl butted in. 'What's it to do with you?'

'But that's my job, Miss Everrett. Liaison. Remember?' He turned back to Downes.

'How are you approaching the story? Because it isn't a very new one, is it?'

'How do you mean?'

Downes leant forward, putting himself more firmly in Barlow's line of vision.

'Well people have been talking about the decline of the mining industry for a good many years now. I wouldn't have thought there was much new to say on the subject.'

'Yes, that's partly true, but the fact that a subject has been dealt with before is not necessarily a reason why it shouldn't be done again.'

The girl was eager to talk once she sensed they were on safe ground. She talked quickly, using her hands now. Barlow, only half listening, watched her face. In repose, it had looked tired and strained, but now it was alive again. She talked with her eyes as well as her voice, concentrating all her attention on him. He squinted at his watch and then forced himself to listen to what she was saying . . .

'. . . and we are still no nearer any real kind of fuel policy. Particularly one that takes in social issues as well. That is what you have to try and assess. How do you measure the cost of coal against the cost of killing a community that has existed for a hundred years?'

Barlow saw the porter approaching. Price was on schedule.

'Mr Downes. There's a telephone call for you – in the lobby.'

With Downes gone the two of them sat in uncompanionable silence. Every few seconds the girl glanced over her shoulder and was not pleased when she saw the porter approaching again.

'Mr Downes asked me to tell you that he had to go out for a few minutes. Some trouble with the equipment, he said. He said there was no need to wait for him and he would see you in the morning.'

'But that's. . . . Thank you very much.'

The girl rose to her feet.

'In that case, Mr Barlow, if you'll excuse me. We have to make an early start.'

'Don't go yet.' It sounded casual but there was an edge to Barlow's voice. 'There's half a glass each left in the bottle.' He leant forward and poured an inch of wine apiece. 'Besides there's still one question I want to ask you.'

'What's that?'

'Well, there are two questions really.'

'Yes?'

'Why you are doing this story now? Why not wait a bit?'

'Why should we wait a bit?'

'If you waited a month Forrester would be out of prison.'

She went very still in her chair. Then gradually her eyes moved to Barlow's face. She sat in complete silence, staring at him, but he could sense her mind flicking quickly through the possibilities: denial, bluff, prevarication, defiance. Barlow suddenly lifted his hand and gave a signal. She spun round in her chair as if expecting to see half a dozen policemen bearing down upon her. Instead the waiter moved obediently over. Barlow indicated the bottle of wine.

'I think we'd like another of these, please. Unless, of course, you'd prefer something stronger?'

She said nothing, so Barlow waved the waiter on his way.

Then came the reaction, and not what he had expected. She was furious.

'How dare you! You sit there like some great big tabby cat. All smug. Thinking you can play with us like a couple of little white mice. Pat us about with your paws until you get bored with your nice game. If you knew what we were doing, why didn't you just say instead of letting us make fools of ourselves like that? You make me sick. You've spent too long pushing people around. People too scared to answer back because you had all the power and they had none. Well, you've got no power over us. We are going to do the Forrester story and just you try and stop us.'

Barlow, in his turn, had gone very still during her tirade. His eyes never left her face. Only his hand clenched around the empty bottle showed that her words were having any effect. The knuckles grew whiter and whiter until, as she finished, he released his hand very slowly and reached forward towards her. She shrank away from him, frightened by the anger in his eyes. But he merely took her glass and set it alongside his. The waiter was coming through the door into the lounge.

They sat in silence as he refilled both glasses.

'Right,' said Barlow as soon as they were left alone again. 'Now I'll tell you what I really came here to talk to you about.'

'I don't want to hear it. I'm going to drink one more glass of wine because I feel like another glass and I don't see why your presence should deprive me of it. And then I am going to bed.'

'There's no hurry. The boy friend won't be back for another quarter of an hour.'

'He is not my "boy friend" as you so quaintly phrase it ... How do you know?'

'Because I arranged to have him,' Barlow waved a hand in a pantomime gesture, 'spirited away. It's the kind of thing you can do if you have power.'

She got to her feet very slowly.

'If you've hurt him, I warn you, I'll . . .'

Barlow gave a bored groan.

'Oh for heaven's sake sit down and stop behaving like a child. Of course I haven't hurt him. Do you suppose I've arranged to have him beaten up in the cells or something? If that's the kind of mature approach they teach you in television, it's no wonder most of it's so bad.'

She sat down again slowly.

'Then where is he?'

'I just arranged for him to go galloping off on a wild goose chase.'

She gave a sigh of relief and reached for her glass. Then she returned to the attack.

'You may be able to make fools of us but you won't stop us doing this story.'

'I know. What is more I wouldn't dream of trying. It would be unprofessional and I should be totally exceeding the limits of my authority.'

This time she looked really startled. Her glass stayed half-way raised to her lips and she stared at Barlow over its rim. Barlow found himself thinking that of all the varied expressions that had crossed her face during the evening this was the one that suited her best. It made her look younger and more vulnerable. The hard edge was gone. Instead she looked appealing.

'But . . . But if you *want* us to do the story, then what are you doing here?'

'I didn't say that. I didn't say that I wanted you to do the story. I said I wouldn't dream of trying to stop you. But, as a matter of fact, I very much hope you won't do it.'

'Why not? Why shouldn't we?'

'Because you won't do any good and you might even do some harm.'

'Oh spare me that old line. You'll be telling me to let sleeping dogs lie next.'

'No. I'm telling you that dogs, sleeping or otherwise, are best left to the dog-handlers.'

'What does that mean?'

'This is a police matter. Leave it to the police.'

'That would suit you very nicely. We pack up and go home. You hold a little private inquiry, hush it all up, whitewash everything in sight and then sit back and relax again. Oh no. We came down here to do a story and we're going to do it.'

'And nothing I can do or say will make you change your mind?'

'Nothing.'

Barlow sat back in his chair and gazed reflectively at the girl. She returned the look with a defiant stare. She was obviously expecting another outburst but as he continued to sit there placidly she began to look slightly uneasy.

'Well?'

'Well what?'

'Shouldn't you be making the speech now about "I can't stop you but just don't ever come to me looking for co-operation on anything else you might want to do"?'

'That isn't one of my speeches.'

'So that's it?'

'It would seem so.'

She stood up and picked up her handbag. 'So I'll go to bed. We've got a lot of work to do tomorrow.'

'Sit down again for a minute.'

'Why? . . . Don't tell me you're going to try a last-minute appeal to my better nature?'

'No, not that.'

Barlow was still sitting easily in his chair looking as relaxed as if he were at home in front of his own fire. Although he had asked her to stay he made no move towards her in support of his words. She stood uncertainly beside her chair. Suddenly Barlow leant forward, with an expansive smile, and poured another glass of wine for them both.

'It's just that you're a very attractive, intelligent girl and I'd hate to think that we were parting company with my last impressions of you as they are.'

'And what are they?'

'I think a fair summing up would be about an equal mixture of mild dislike and absolute contempt.'

Barlow's manner had been so bland and benevolent that it was a second before the words got through. When they did, however, her face flushed red and she sat down with a bump. Barlow watched her fighting for control and winning. Her voice when it finally emerged was icily cold.

'I think perhaps it might be a good idea if you explained just what you mean.'

'All right. I will. You've been sitting there masquerading as a champion of truth, the defender of the people and the living embodiment of what you and your kind call "The right to know". At the same time you've been waving about a mass of half-baked, ridiculous prejudices and silly, juvenile attitudes. You pretend to care about the truth. You couldn't care less about the truth. All you're interested in is playing your own silly game of cowboys and Indians. You're like kids rushing around throwing stones through windows and then trying to pretend that what you're really doing is letting in the fresh air. You make me sick.'

All this was delivered in the same amiable tone as if he had been outlining his plans for a pleasant evening. As he finished, the girl opened her mouth to speak, but Barlow held up a hand in an extremely policeman-like gesture.

'No, I haven't finished. Now you may not have liked what I have just said but you can still listen to what I'm going to say next. And this is official. You were using silly words like "white-wash" earlier on. Well, I am now informing you that on the basis of what I have heard this evening – not from you but from a policeman who knows what he is talking about – I mean to ensure that a full enquiry will be held into the arrest and conviction of James Forrester. Unofficially – and entirely off the record – I think there was a gross miscarriage of justice. I don't like that. It offends me – as a man and as a policeman. And I propose to do something about it. Now if you start poking around asking questions, all you will do is get in the way. But if you leave it to me I will take that case apart and I will find out just exactly what did happen. And if anyone is guilty, whether police officers or not, then believe you me by the time I've finished with them they'll wish they had never been born. And that is a promise . . . Now it's your turn.'

As he sat back, Barlow saw that he had achieved the result he had wanted. The girl, having been in a fury, was now so confused by his sudden switch of tactics that she was no longer sure of her reaction. He leant forward and took her hand.

'I'm sorry, love. I didn't mean to be rough with you. I know you get involved and I believe you when you say you really do care. But just trust me. That's all I ask. I can call on resources that aren't available to you. It's a part of my job and, believe me, I intend to do it. So – trust me?'

He could see the struggle in the girl's face and, for a few seconds, he wondered whether he was going to win. But then she smiled, somewhat ruefully but nevertheless a smile, and Barlow barely suppressed a sigh of relief. For a moment he thought he had played his ace too soon.

'All right,' she said. 'I will. But will you back me up when I tell the others why we aren't doing the story?'

'Of course I will. I'll tell them exactly what I've told you. Well . . . an edited version anyway.'

She gave him a rather battered smile.

'There is one other thing I would like.'

'Yes. What's that?'

'Could I have another glass of wine?'

Barlow grinned and reached for the bottle. He filled their glasses and hitched his chair closer towards her.

'A toast,' he said, raising his glass. 'To . . . let me think . . . to . . . television liaison.'

He saluted her with a flourish.

'There are moments when a policeman's lot is not entirely an unhappy one.'

She inclined her head in mock graciousness.

'Thank you kindly, sir.'

She realised she was still clutching her handbag and put it down on the chair beside her. Barlow looked around and caught the eye of the waiter who was still propping up a pillar at the far end of the lounge.

'I think that I should like to complete the evening with a glass of brandy. Would you care to join me?'

'That would be very nice.'

They sat in comfortable silence as Barlow gave the order and until the waiter returned with the two goblets.

'Will you be wanting anything else this evening, sir?'

'If you mean is it all right for you to push off, the answer is yes.'

'Thank you, sir.'

Barlow waited until he had gone and then looked around.

'Well, it's just us.'

'So it seems. I wonder what happened to my poor director.'

'I'm sorry about that.'

'Don't lie. You're not sorry at all.'

'All right. I'm not sorry . . . What shall we talk about?'

'Anything. Anything that isn't television or police-work.'

'I know. Let's talk about you.'

'That's funny. I was going to suggest we talked about you.'

'I said it first. Anyway, there's one thing I've wanted to know about you . . . oh, practically ever since I first saw you this morning in the canteen.'

'Oh, what's that?'

Barlow leant forward and picked up his brandy glass.

'Why are you paying fifty pounds a week to a blackmailer?'

'You bastard!'

It was touch and go whether he got her drink in his face. Barlow saw her fingers clench round the bowl of the glass as it lifted and he got ready to duck. Instead, the hand relaxed, her shoulders slumped a little and she began to cry. Barlow sat quietly waiting. After a few minutes the sobbing began to subside, and he reached forward and put a handkerchief in her hand. She flung it down violently, which he took as a sign that a complete recovery was not far away.

'No, not a bastard,' he said. 'A policeman. Always remember that.'

She didn't answer but instead groped for her brandy and gulped defiantly.

'Listen,' he said as gently as he could manage while still pressing his advantage. 'I won't insult you by asking you to think of me as a friend or any rubbish like that. I am a policeman. And I want you to think of me as one. You don't need a friend; you need a policeman. I know you're being blackmailed and I can stop it. Tell me a few things I need to know and I can pick up a phone and stop it – just like that.'

'Oh, you are powerful, aren't you?' It was an attempt at a sneer but there was no enthusiasm in the effort. Barlow took the remark at its face value.

'Yes. I am. In certain areas – and crime is one of them. And that's what we are talking about. So tell me. First of all – how?'

She wasn't a girl who cried prettily and delicately. Instead she sniffed – loudly. She groped for the handkerchief, found it where it lay on one of the chairs and blew her nose.

'I can't tell you.'

'You mean you won't.'

'If you like.'

'No, I don't like. So I'll tell you. Photographs. Yes? Am I right?'

She nodded.

'And an offer to post them to your husband?'

She nodded again and shut her eyes involuntarily, as if to shut out the pictures and the sight of her husband's face as he looked at them.

'Forgive me saying this,' Barlow sounded oddly diffident. 'But I get the impression that yours is a . . . well, what's called a modern marriage. Would it be so totally disastrous if your husband knew you'd been unfaithful to him?'

She shook her head violently.

'No, it's not that so much. He might be upset, but no, you're right, no, it's not that. It's just that they weren't . . . The man in the pictures . . .'

'I know. He wasn't really the sort of man your husband would think you found at all attractive. Obvious, crude, vulgar – not your "sort" at all.'

She looked at him in astonishment.

'How did you know?'

'Because,' Barlow heard a voice in his head saying, 'I've been a policeman for a long time and everything has a pattern and once you spot the pattern it all slots together in much the same way and there is nothing really new under the sun and no one is really any different from all the others however much they like to think they are.' . . . But he didn't say any of it. Instead he looked at the crumpled, slightly forlorn figure in the chair opposite.

'You want it to stop, don't you?'

'Oh yes.'

'All right. I know it isn't easy for you to tell me, sitting like this. But write it down for me. Make it a letter. Go up to your room now and write it. Just put it all down. You'll feel better just for doing that. And leave it for me at the reception desk. But do it now. Make sure the letter gets down to the desk first thing in the morning, otherwise I shan't get it.'

'Why? Are you leaving?'

'Yes. I'm going back to London.'

'Why?'

'Well, for a number of reasons. But mainly because I wish to talk to a gentleman called Fenton.'

6

Barlow read her letter over a cup of coffee in a plastic pull-up on the M4 back to London. The letter had been waiting for him at reception but he had slid it unopened into his pocket, made one telephone call to his office and driven rapidly away. Now, an hour later, he looked at the closely typed sheet of paper in his hand.

'Dear Mr Barlow, You were quite right. I am going to find this much easier than talking to you. I suppose you knew that because of people writing statements or confessions. Don't be afraid that I shan't think of you as a policeman, by the way. You've given me too many opportunities to do just that. Still, you wanted to know, so I might as well tell you.

'It wasn't very important. It wasn't even very unusual. It was a story about young militants. We had one or two contacts and we were following them up. One of the places we went to was a flat in Fulham. There was a party going on there. I met this man. I suppose he thought I was more interested in him than I really was because I was so interested in finding out how active they were. Well, I found out, although not quite in the way I intended to. It was late and I had had a fair amount to drink and . . . oh, anyway, I went back to his flat with him. I didn't feel very proud of myself the morning after and I got out very quickly and made some excuse in order to drop out of doing the story.

'And then, a month later the pictures arrived. They weren't pretty. They had been taken while I was asleep but he was posing with me. What was nasty was that they were deliberately designed to humiliate me and make me look cheap and to have the same effect on anyone who knew me. So you see, that is why I could never tell Simon, my husband. He's very sweet and I'm very fond of him but he hasn't exactly had a wide experience of the seamier side of life. He isn't very tough either and you would have to be very tough indeed to cope with these. And I know it would hurt him terribly.

'I'm sorry. It's getting very late and I'm very tired and this letter isn't very well written. But I can't risk anything happening, so please, Mr Barlow, don't do anything. Forget you're a policeman just for once and let me alone. It isn't too much money and they haven't ever asked for more. I'm not quite sure why, really. A man did phone me up once when I was a bit late sending the money and said something about being very gentle with me because they wanted to keep me in good condition. But I don't know whether it was just a nasty joke or what. Anyway, I haven't heard anything from them since. So please, won't you pretend you never found out?'

At that point, with only a scrawled signature the letter stopped abruptly. Barlow smiled rather sadly to himself. 'Yes,' he murmured under his breath. 'I wondered when that particular penny was going to drop.' Then the smile left his face as suddenly as if a hand had wiped it away. Instead his mouth settled into a hard line. He finished his coffee abruptly, got up and marched out to his car. An hour and a half later he drew up outside the television studios.

Ten minutes after that he sat in front of a desk trying to sum up the man who sat opposite him. John Henderson, the head of the department, had looked mildly surprised when Barlow announced that he would like to have a chat with the department's administration assistant, but had been too polite to comment. So Barlow found himself ushered into this office and introduced to Mr Kendrick, who now spoke in a rather self-important, fussy manner.

'Well, Chief Superintendent, what kind of information precisely did you wish me to reveal to you? Nothing confidential, I hope? Nobody's been cooking the books around here?'

Kendrick took his glasses off, polished them vigorously on his tie and put them on again, a manoeuvre he had already repeated three times since Barlow had been in the room. For a moment, Barlow wondered whether to keep up the pretence or not. Then he thought of Fenton sitting in the middle of his spider's web a few miles away and decided to settle for results.

'Yes.'

The word hit the desk between them with a dull thud. Kendrick blinked, reached for his glasses, thought better of it and blinked again.

'I beg your pardon?'

'I said yes. Somebody has ... been cooking the books.'

'But ... I'm afraid I don't follow you. I understood from Mr Henderson's introductory remarks that you were here in some kind of purely informal, liaison capacity. Surely, if that is so, then any such remark as the one you have just made would be totally improper, apart of course from being so unlikely as to be ... well ... laughable.'

Barlow allowed the convoluted sentence to flow gently past him.

'Mr Kendrick, I am a policeman.' He seemed to have been saying that quite a lot recently, he thought. 'As a policeman, if I come across evidence of criminal activity, it is my duty to take appropriate action whatever the circumstances.'

He sat back rather smugly with the air of one who has returned an unfamiliar service rather creditably. Unfortunately, Mr Kendrick took his elaborate formality as an invitation to carry on with the ritual.

'I appreciate that, Mr Barlow and may I say that as a private citizen I applaud such diligence, but obviously I have an equal, if not greater, responsibility in my official capacity within this organisation. I am bound to regard that responsibility as taking precedence in this particular case. In view of this, I would obviously require you to make any approach on such a matter through the proper channels.'

'You mean that if I asked you to let me have a look at one or two of your files, privately, you would turn me down?'

'Yes.' For once Kendrick was shocked into saying what he meant. 'I should.'

'That would be a pity, Mr Kendrick.'

'Well, I'm sorry, Chief Superintendent. I assure you that I have no desire to seem obstructive, but you must appreciate that I am obliged to follow established procedures.'

'I didn't mean it was a pity from my point of view, I meant it was a pity from yours.'

'What do you mean?'

Kendrick's elegant manner was melting like a snowman in hot sun.

'I mean that since you won't help me informally, I shall have to proceed formally.'

'But that is precisely what I was suggesting, Mr Barlow. An approach through the proper channels from your people to my people . . .'

Kendrick's rapid attempt to scramble back in control died as Barlow held up a hand.

'No, Mr Kendrick. I shall get up from here, walk down the road to the local police station, inform them that I have reason to believe a criminal offence has been committed and that the relevant information is in this office, and in two hours you'll have a detective constable and a raw aide-to-CID tramping all over the place . . .'

'That couldn't happen.'

Barlow smiled. 'Perhaps I was exaggerating a little. But I could easily get you subpoenaed to produce the books in a court of law.'

He sat back and stared ostentatiously out of the window at a pigeon on a nearby roof. The pigeon, obviously suffering from a guilty conscience, flew away immediately. Barlow looked back into the room. Kendrick caught his eye and, putting his hands flat on the desk in front of him, rose slowly to his feet.

'Which files do you want to see, Mr Barlow?'

Barlow told him, and, after setting them out on the desk, Kendrick excused himself and left him alone. It took Chief Superintendent Barlow just twenty minutes to find what he was looking for.

7

'My dear Barlow, you have been busy.'

Fenton was being as urbane as usual. He leant back in his chair, put his fingertips together and regarded Barlow with slightly wary pride – the kind of look one gives a pet retriever who has been after a rabbit and brought back the neighbour's cat.

'I've never seen much point in hanging about.'

Barlow, as so often in his conversations with Fenton, found himself driven back on the simple, straightforward pose. It occurred to him that each of them was under no illusion about the nature of the game.

'So you've established blackmail,' Fenton was doing what he called 'pulling the threads together' ... 'But you didn't get a name from her? Why not? Surely not from a sense of chivalry at pressing a lady too far?'

'Not likely. I knew I would only get the name if I could give a guarantee in return and I wasn't in a position to do that – then.'

'Quite. Very sensible. What about the other side of the balance-sheet?'

'I got that ... From the records of payments on the film side of the programme. It was very easy. Any decent auditor would spot it in ten minutes if he was looking for it. She's obviously told her director some story or he's in love with her and does what she tells him. This is the way it works – all film equipment, cameras, lights and so on are usually provided by the film department. But on every story those two go on there is always an invoice for additional lighting. It's not unusual, apparently. Lights are heavy things to lug around everywhere, so people quite often hire extra ones just for something specific. But never as regularly as this. The invoices are always made out to one hire company, never mind where they happen to be filming. They are submitted separately and paid separately. I've had the address checked out – it's a tobacconist not far from where the lady lives. He takes letters for people. It's dishonest and, since she endorses the cheques with an assumed name before paying them into her account, it's positive deception, but at least she isn't making any really personal profit. The sum involved always works out at exactly the blackmail money she needs – £200 a month.'

Fenton looked slightly pained. 'It seems somewhat crude to me.'

'Yes but it's simple and it works.'

'Or rather it did until you arrived on the scene . . . Well, I must say that all seems quite satisfactory. All we have to do is remove that rather unpleasant young man from the lady's life and we can all give ourselves a pat on the back.'

Fenton started rearranging piles of paper on his desk, his usual form of shorthand when he wished to bring proceedings rapidly to a close. Barlow leant over and picked up his briefcase.

'We still have to establish the young man's identity, of course.'

'Yes of course.' Fenton thought for a moment. 'Perhaps it might be as well if you did that, since you seem to have established some form of rapport with the lady. Find out. Let me know. And you can wash your hands of the whole thing.'

Barlow got to his feet. 'Who's the Pilate here? You or me?'

Fenton paused. 'Both of us, I hope.'

'Speak for yourself.'

'In other quarters – on high as it were – I have to speak for both of us.'

'That seems fine,' said Barlow, 'but shall I charge the girl or do you want the local station to do it?'

Fenton carefully straightened his copy of *The Times* and moved it from one side of the desk to the other. Without looking up he said:

'Sit down, Charles. You make me nervous when you loom over me.'

Barlow sat down on the edge of his seat. Fenton eventually finished landscaping his desk and looked up.

'How long have you been here with us?'

'Nine months or so.'

'Tell me – do you still miss the more straightforward police-work? The old routine of Thamesford?'

'Sometimes. It had its compensations. I like things to be . . . straightforward.'

'Yes, I realise that. On the other hand, Charles, in this building and particularly in this room things very seldom are. Though I do have a passion for neatness.'

Fenton leant forward and carefully straightened a fountain pen that had been lying some ten degrees out of true.

'I like things to be neat as well. I also like them to be finished.'

Fenton brightened up considerably.

'I'm glad we agree, Charles . . . So we can regard that as settled?'

'Certainly. I'll get tabs on the bloke, arrange to have him picked up. And I'll charge the girl.'

A lesser man than Fenton would have sighed. As it was, his eyelids lowered fractionally in what passed for him as a dramatic gesture.

'Charles, you almost persuade me that you have some grudge against the lady. Could it be that you succumbed to her charms but she somehow failed to appreciate yours?'

With an effort Barlow kept his voice level.

'No, I wasn't trying. And if I had been, I like to think it

wouldn't have influenced my actions. And while we're about it I regard the suggestion as extremely offensive.'

Suddenly Fenton's face cracked into a grin. Barlow blinked in astonishment. It was a bit like seeing the Mona Lisa stick out her tongue.

'Charles, you've been here too long.'

Barlow stiffened and got to his feet.

'In that case I'd be only too happy to be relieved of my duties and go back to my previous post.'

'Oh sit down, sit down.' Fenton waved his hand in apology. 'I didn't mean it like that. It's simply that you're beginning to talk like me. Three months ago, if I had made a remark like that, you would have offered to knock my teeth down my throat.'

He got up and drifted towards a cupboard on the wall.

'Allow me to offer you a glass of sherry as a token of remorse.'

He poured two glasses and offered one to Barlow who eyed the pale liquid with total lack of enthusiasm. As far as Barlow was concerned, alcohol divided into three categories: beer, whisky, and rough, red wine. He appreciated that Fenton was making a gesture but he would have preferred it in some more substantial form. Fenton sipped the sherry and eyed Barlow over the glass.

'You have done extremely well, Charles. I am very grateful to you. I would be even more grateful if you now allowed this matter to rest. I need hardly assure you that I have a very good reason for asking.'

'I'm sure you have. But I'm sorry, I can't.'

'Can't, Charles? Or won't?'

'Both.'

Fenton's voice became even silkier.

'I have made you a request. I prefer, on the whole, to deal with my colleagues on this basis. Provided, of course, they do appreciate the – shall we say – the strength of a request when I make it directly.'

'I understand that. But I deal in facts. The fact is that the girl has committed an offence. It's at least criminal deception under

Section 15 of the Theft Act. It's a police matter and I am a policeman.'

'You have no need to remind me. I have been forcibly aware of it for some time now. You are also, although it grieves me to have to point it out, working for me. And I'm calling you off.'

'No.'

'What do you mean, no?'

Fenton's bland, languid manner vanished. Barlow suddenly saw why he had such a reputation for ruthless action when the need arose. But he battled grimly on.

'I'm not a dog. And this isn't a rabbit. I don't work that way. I never have and I won't start now. I will carry out your instructions but I will not bend the rules just to suit some politician's convenience.'

Fenton was leaning back in his chair again. The pose had been carefully slipped back over his shoulders.

'So, would I be correct in assuming that, however I phrased my request to you not to do so, you would nevertheless go ahead and charge this girl?'

'Yes. Or at least see she was charged.'

Fenton got up and poured himself another glass of sherry. He proferred the decanter to Barlow who shook his head.

'Do you know, Charles, I find myself thinking sometimes that life was much easier when I dealt with quiet, docile civil servants. They never argued except in the politest way. And they never put pressure on me in the crude but effective way you are doing now.'

'I beg your pardon?'

'Spare me the bland, innocent look. It doesn't suit you. You know and I know that you couldn't care less whether that girl is charged or not. You are a dog and this is a rabbit. But you've seen a bigger rabbit somewhere further down the burrow.'

Fenton turned on his heel, walked over to the window and stood staring down into the street. His back did not invite comment and Barlow didn't offer any. Suddenly Fenton swung on his heel.

'All right. It wasn't what I or my masters originally had in mind. But it's your rabbit. Talk to the girl, get a name from her and have him picked up. Quickly. Tonight, in fact. And hold him. The moment you've got him, phone me. I'll be here. And I'll arrange for one of our friends from down the road to tell you not only what he thinks your rabbit looks like but what kind of creature he is.'

'Oh.' Barlow looked taken aback. 'It's like that is it?'

'Yes, it's like that.'

An unbiased observer might have been forgiven for thinking that Fenton sounded irritated. Barlow decided to beat a tactful retreat. His hand was on the door when Fenton spoke:

'Charles?'

'Yes?'

'You wanted it. You've got it. So make sure you get it right, won't you?'

Barlow nodded and the door shut behind him. Fenton sat staring at it for some considerable time and then reached out a hand for the phone – the red phone. He gave an extension number and then started to talk to the voice at the other end. The voice sounded very worried indeed.

PART II

8

Barlow arranged to meet Maggie Everrett in a restaurant just off Kensington High Street which specialised in looking like a gloomy Victorian parlour. However, it had two considerable advantages: the food was reasonably good and the tables were far enough apart for private conversations to remain private. It had taken him an hour to track her down and a good many minutes to persuade her that they did have urgent unfinished business.

They made fairly strained conversation in the intervals between courses. Now, over coffee, Barlow leant forward and lit her cigarette.

'Let's talk business. I read your letter and I want to thank you for writing it. It can't have been easy. But I am afraid I need to know more.'

'There isn't any more. I told you all about it.'

'I want the name of the man and any information you may have as to where I can find him.'

'What will you do with it when you've got it?'

'I shall go and collect him – or rather I'll arrange to have it done. Then you can forget all about it.'

She gave a wry smile.

'I don't think I'll ever be able to do that.'

'Perhaps not. But he won't bother you any more.'

'Oh yes, he will. Well, perhaps he won't. But there will be others. Once a thing like that starts, you can't stop it.'

Barlow leaned forward and tapped her arm. She looked up to find him folding his hands in the manner of someone preparing to deliver an address.

'The main thing to remember about being a television reporter is the importance of communicating with an audience. You must be prepared to share your enthusiasm and sense of involvement with them.'

He paused and looked expectantly at her.

'What *are* you talking about?'

'I am talking nonsense to you about your business. It makes a change from listening to you talking nonsense about mine.'

She managed to force a laugh, although not a cheerful one, and Barlow dropped his lecturer pose.

'Now listen to me. I'm a cop. I am also a tough cop, and, though I say it myself, a good one. You know I'm tough – you've had a taste of it. You'll have to take my word for it that I'm good. I can also get action when I want it and how I want it.'

'Could you get us more coffee then?'

Barlow hesitated and then grinned at her.

'At least I prefer you cheeky to depressed. Be a good girl. Tell me who the fellow is and I promise you we'll stop all this nonsense for good.'

'Promises, promises . . .'

'All right.' Barlow was getting annoyed. He wasn't used to having to work so hard in order to carry conviction.

'I'll guarantee it. You want the photographs and the negatives. Right? If you can tell me where I can find this feller, then I'll do the rest. Now.'

She looked at him steadily, appraisingly. He made no attempt to persuade her further. But suddenly, for the first time, she found his square, solid frame reassuring rather than worrying. He read her mind because he suddenly reached out and patted her hand.

'That's right, love. I'm on your side now.'

She smiled back.

'All right. Do you want to write it down?'

By way of reply, Barlow produced an ordinary police pocket-book with a pencil tucked into it. He extracted the pencil and held it poised.

'His name is Bruce Gregory. The address is 49 Arundel Crescent. It's in Fulham. It's a big house and a number of them share it. A sort of commune. I think they're still there because somebody on the programme was talking about them the other week. They'd been involved in some row about illegal picketing.'

Barlow got up. She got the impression that he had moved into another gear. The waiter was just passing and Barlow took him by the arm.

'A phone I could use.'

The waiter smiled and pointed towards the back of the restaurant. Barlow looked down at her, nodded reassuringly and walked briskly away. She saw him pick up the phone and dial. He appeared to get through at once and she saw him talk quickly and urgently for no more than a minute. He put the phone down and, on his way back, said something to the waiter. Then he was sitting opposite her and she could see him deliberately relaxing again.

'I asked the waiter for more coffee and two brandies. All right?'

She nodded.

'What happens now?'

'We wait. Unless you want to come and watch?'

'I don't want to see . . .'

Barlow made an impatient movement.

'I didn't say that. I'm not involved in this exercise and I don't want to be. But you might as well come along. Then you can be sure everything's all right.'

He got up and went over to the phone again. This time he spoke only a couple of sentences. When he got back to the table, he reached down for his brandy and drank it off without sitting down.

'Drink yours. Otherwise we'll be too late.'

She scrambled to her feet and got her coat on while Barlow paid the bill. As they left the restaurant she said:

'Where's your car parked?'

'I haven't got one.'

'Oh. I'm afraid I didn't bring mine. Shall we go over to the hotel? There are sometimes taxis there.'

'No. We'll just stand here.'

She tugged at his arm.

'But we'll never get a cab here. They all go straight past and down into the High Street.'

He looked down at her.

'We don't need a taxi. All we do is stand here for another' – he looked at his watch – 'thirty seconds.'

She looked puzzled but he didn't add anything. Instead, he carried on looking at his watch. Eventually he murmured half to himself.

'About now, I should think.'

As he spoke a white Jaguar turned the corner, travelling very fast indeed, and slid to a halt with its rear door almost precisely opposite Barlow. The car had no markings, and an immaculately turned-out young man got out of the driving seat and came round to them.

'Mr Barlow? I'm DC Frost, sir.'

'Right,' said Barlow. They got in.

'You know where?'

'Yes, sir.'

As the driver answered the car was already moving. It hovered briefly at the corner and then accelerated smoothly and very fast down Kensington High Street. Maggie summoned up her courage to ask a question.

'I thought police cars had lights and bells and things.'

Barlow spoke to the driver.

'Perhaps you would enlighten the lady?'

'These cars don't, miss. We find it less conspicuous.'

He then swirled the car into the North End Road and sent it

heading south at seventy miles an hour. Maggie found herself thinking that there was more than one way of drawing attention to yourself. Barlow took pity on her bewilderment.

'You're the guest of the Flying Squad, Miss Everrett. Otherwise known as the Heavy Mob.'

He leant forward to the driver.

'How long?'

'Less than two minutes from here, sir,' answered the driver. He swept past a lorry and started a complicated and dodg'em-like progress through the back streets of Fulham. Maggie assumed her nervousness was communicating itself because the driver suddenly half turned his head towards her with a grin.

'It's all right, miss. I'm a Class One driver.'

Barlow leant towards Maggie.

'Being translated that means he's almost certainly better than anyone you've ever driven with before.'

Maggie looked at him and then despite herself laughed.

'All right, damn you. I'm impressed. What else happened when you waved your little wand?'

Barlow opened his mouth to answer but the car radio spoke briskly.

'Mobile Four. Do we wait or go in?'

Barlow leaned over from the back seat. The driver handed him the microphone.

'Carry on. I'm just here for the ride.'

The radio quacked a 'Very good, sir' at him. The driver took the microphone back from Barlow.

'Where do you want us, sir?'

'Somewhere out of the way but with a good view.'

As he spoke they slid smoothly round yet another corner and ahead of them saw two similar cars and a police van drawn up on the opposite side of the road. The driver slid into the kerb fifty yards away from them, cut his engine and flicked his lights. A policeman on the pavement glanced towards them but made no sign that he had registered their arrival. They sat for a moment or two and then the door of the house opened and dark blue figures began shepherding other figures out and into the van. A dog-handler and an Alsatian stood alongside looking bored.

Suddenly one of the men broke free and started to run across the street. Maggie heard herself shouting.

'He's getting away.'

Neither Barlow nor the driver moved although the man was running towards them. She didn't see anything happen but suddenly the dog was loping along at the man's heels. As he came within a few yards of them, the dog leapt and sent him sprawling on the pavement. His arms waved as he struggled and then suddenly lay still. The dog stood with its paws straddled and its head lowered, its jaws a few inches above his face. The man began to scream.

Maggie found herself fumbling for the car door. Barlow's hand reached across and fastened over hers.

'Stay in the car.'

His voice cracked like a whip in her ear and she sank back on the seat. The dog-handler had been strolling along the pavement. As he reached the spot, he spoke quietly to the dog which stepped contemptuously aside. It stood never taking its eyes off the man as he lay there. The dog-handler reached down, jerked him to his feet and pushed him in the direction of the van. They watched as he was bundled in. Then a uniformed inspector appeared in the doorway. The policeman outside jerked his head towards the squad car, and he came over to it. As he drew near, Barlow wound down his window. The inspector bent his head.

'Evening, sir. Would this be what you were looking for, sir?'

He handed a battered foolscap envelope into the car. Without a word Barlow passed them to Maggie, leant forward and switched an interior light on and then studiously stared out of the window. Maggie, after a moment, spoke in a whisper.

'Yes.'

The inspector nodded.

'We'll double-check, sir. We also have the man you were inquiring about.'

'Good.' Barlow thought for a moment.

'I need them held for a couple of hours. But not for that.' He indicated the envelope which Maggie was holding. 'For something else. Any drugs?'

'There'll be no trouble about holding them, sir.'

There was an odd note in the inspector's voice. Barlow looked a question.

'We found six of these on the premises.'

The inspector reached into the pocket of his coat and produced a dark object. He held it under the light of the car for Barlow to see. It was a revolver. There was silence while Barlow, the inspector and the driver all regarded it with interest. Finally, it was Barlow who spoke:

'But I thought they were just a bunch of . . .'

His voice trailed off as he flapped his hand in a dismissive way.

'Yes, sir,' said the inspector. 'They are. But they seem to have developed a new style.'

'Mmmm.' Barlow stroked his chin, then leant forward to the driver.

'Right. Home Office.' To the inspector. 'Thanks very much. Lock them all up. But don't talk to them. I'll be down later. And I want them nice and fresh. I'll phone you when I'm on my way.'

He wound up the window and the driver slipped through the gears as the Jaguar started to accelerate away. Barlow turned to Maggie.

'The driver will take you home. If there are any more copies of those about they'll find them and I'll make sure they're destroyed. I'm sorry I can't take you back myself.' He smiled at her. 'Don't worry. You've got those and Sonny Boy isn't going to shoot his mouth off. I'll see to that.'

'Where are you going?'

'Back to the office.'

Barlow leant forward to the driver.

'Pass a message. Mr Fenton's office. Tell him I'm on my way.

And tell him I've found a rabbit with interesting habits. And make this car move.'

'Yes, sir.'

The car, which had been travelling at seventy, shot forward. The driver reached for the microphone as Maggie shut her eyes.

9

Fenton had company. He did not introduce Barlow but merely nodded towards an empty chair. Then he turned to the other man.

'This is Barlow. I should be grateful if you would provide him with as much assistance as possible.'

It was an extremely stiff and formal request even for Fenton, so Barlow examined the stranger with renewed interest. He was in his late thirties, dressed in a T-shirt, faded and torn jeans, sandals, and carrying a rather expensive suede satchel. His hair was well over his shoulders. He caught Barlow looking at the bag and suddenly grinned.

'I stole it, man.'

His voice didn't match the dress. It was distinctly Eton and Oxford. He waved a hand at the rest of his clothes.

'I apologise for arriving in my working gear. I gathered it was rather urgent.'

Fenton looked at the sandals and the bare, rather dirty toes that poked out of them.

'Don't you find those chilly?'

'Extremely. But we are all, from time to time, called upon to make sacrifices for our Queen and country. It so happens mine are going to be chilblains . . .' He turned to Barlow.

'You mentioned something about "interesting habits".'

Barlow glanced at Fenton who was carefully lining up two pencils an inch apart. He looked up.

'This gentleman is employed by the establishment I mentioned earlier. We have undertaken to co-operate with them fully. In return for a similar undertaking.' He pushed the pencils aside. 'So let's get on with it.'

Barlow straightened in his chair. If Fenton was making his desk untidy and speaking in words of one syllable, then the matter was serious.

He turned to the other man. 'That lot are politicals. Meetings, power to the people, Socialist Weeklies outside factory gates. Marbles under police-horses' hooves, perhaps, now and again, a bit of industrial sabotage and a home-made bomb. Yes?'

All he got in return was a level stare.

'You're telling me.'

'During tonight's search of the premises, six revolvers were found.'

The gentleman in the sandals reached into his pocket and pulled out an extremely dirty folded rag. He put it on the desk and flipped it open.

'Like that?'

The gun, unlike the rag, was new and clean. Barlow glanced at it.

'That's right.'

Fenton stared at the gun with distaste.

'When I joined this admirable service I had visions of writing impeccable minutes with an elegant quill pen and eating Stilton cheese in the Athenaeum.'

He made to prod at the gun with a tentative finger, but the man in the sandals had wrapped it up and slid it back into his pocket. He leant forward and started to talk.

'You're quite right. These particular rabbits are developing some odd habits, and keeping odd company. As you will know, members of extremist political organisations are kept under general surveillance. Not by us – by the Special Branch. Nothing elaborate. But we like to know vaguely what they are up to. The one thing they don't normally do is talk to each other. Members of extremist left-wing groups usually hate each other more than they hate the bourgeoisie. But one thing they certainly do not do is talk to extremely right-wing figures or to professional criminals. They live worlds apart.'

He stopped and reached in his other pocket. From it he drew an elaborately battered cigarette machine. He stared at it with distaste and then fished out a half-empty packet of tobacco. Fenton leant forward.

'I think possibly in the privacy of this room you might lower your ... er ... front just an inch or so and have a proper cigarette.'

He pushed the box across.

'Thank you. Actually it's not the cigarettes I mind so much. Even these are out of character but I couldn't give up altogether. But eating macrobiotic lunches is driving me spare. Last week I travelled all the way out to Ongar on the tube to go and have a steak and chips for lunch ... Where was I? ... Oh yes ... During the last couple of months, certain individuals from these various groups have been behaving rather oddly. They've been meeting each other, taking considerable care not to be seen doing so. That would be interesting enough. But on one or two occasions there has also been present at these meetings a leading political figure of extreme right-wing views, and a prominent South London criminal. I'm sorry if that sounds a bit like a plot for a bad film but that is what has been happening.'

Barlow leant forward. 'The politician must be Wheeler. Who is the criminal?'

The man smiled. 'In pastures green ...'

'Not Meadows?'

Fenton broke in sharply.

'You sound surprised.'

'I am.' Barlow turned towards him. 'Meadows is, as our friend observed, a prominent criminal. He is also an extremely practical one. He is interested only in projects which guarantee results. He invests his time, money and efforts as shrewdly as any merchant banker. In fact, probably rather more so.'

'In other words, his presence in itself would indicate that the matter is serious.'

Barlow thought for a moment before speaking.

'If you are asking my professional opinion as a policeman ... yes, very serious indeed.'

Fenton looked down at his desk and, with an offended grimace, straightened his pencils again. He turned to the man in sandals.

'I think, in that case, you had better tell us what these people are up to.'

The man leant forward and stubbed his cigarette out.

'That's the trouble, I'm afraid. We don't know.'

'No idea at all?'

There was a sharp edge to Barlow's voice.

'No.'

'But you must have some idea. You're not getting chilblains for fun – and with your sources.'

'No idea.'

The answer was flat and emphatic. The three men sat and looked at each other for a moment and then the man in the sandals spoke again.

'Normally that world has got as many leaks in it as an old tin can. They all gossip and chatter, and we just let our ears flap and occasionally we catch something that sounds a bit silly, so we do something about it. It isn't serious. But this time it's different. All the people involved are hand-picked. They keep their mouths shut. They meet each other, they talk and they go their own ways again. They've been meeting for two months now and we're no nearer finding out why than we were then.'

'So you want us to have a go?'

'Yes. There's a criminal involved. And a big one. Perhaps there might be a way in there.'

'That way's not going to be easy.' Barlow looked thoughtful. 'That gentleman doesn't exactly shout his plans from the roof-tops.'

There was another silence. Suddenly Barlow broke it.

'You say this is a silly world, just talk and nonsense?'

'Yes.'

'So why are you so worried. Just because they've started meeting with a criminal figure?'

'No. It may be a nonsense world. But not everybody in it is a nonsense. It does contain extremely competent, ruthless and violent men. They believe the end justifies the means and they set no limit on the means. This group consists of most of those men.'

Barlow looked at Fenton.

'What about this politician?'

Fenton opened his mouth to speak but the other man cut in.

'He's not important. The fact that he is there is interesting. But he's not a man of action or a man to initiate action. He must be needed for a reason but he isn't the instigator.'

'In that case,' Barlow said, as much to himself as to the others, '... you used the phrase "hand-picked". If these men have been hand-picked ... who picked them?'

The man in sandals got to his feet.

'That's the other worry ... We don't know that either. But whoever did must have something very interesting indeed in mind ...'

10

The police cell in Fulham was colder than Fenton's room but Barlow had the same sense that he was staring at a blank wall. In this case the wall was a tired green whereas Fenton had Ministry of Works wallpaper with a geometric pattern on it. Barlow stopped looking at the wall and took another glance at the man who sat opposite him. He wasn't very impressed by Bruce Gregory. Instead of concentrating on the purpose of the investigation, Barlow found himself wondering what on earth the girl had seen in him. He supposed it was part of the new fashion which dictated that attractive men had to be extremely thin, extremely pale, and extremely boring . . . in which case, thought Barlow, he personally faced a very unpromising future. He went back to looking at the wall again. Eventually, after five minutes had gone very slowly by, Gregory broke the silence.

'I want to know why you're keeping me here.'

His voice was surprisingly deep. His accent was faintly Birmingham overlaid with standard English. According to the information Barlow had acquired before making his way here, he was from Edgbaston and from a fairly comfortable background. At university he had decided that the revolution needed his services and since then he had been involved in fringe activities at an experimental theatre. The only time the man in sandals had allowed any active distaste to creep into his voice had been when he had described to Barlow a play he had seen there. Barlow had gathered that most of the action consisted of a girl counting the whiskers on a tabby cat while a man took all his clothes off. Gregory repeated his question.

'Why am I being kept here?'

Barlow slowly turned away from the wall, looked at him, then turned back to stare at the wall again. Another five minutes went by. Finally, Barlow got up, walked around the table and stood beside him. Gregory kept staring straight ahead, but Barlow could feel the tension as he forced himself not to look up. They stayed like that for a while and then Barlow said casually:

'Was she good in bed?'

Gregory jumped in his seat but Barlow slammed a hand down onto his shoulder. 'No, on second thoughts, don't bother to tell me. I just thought I'd like to know whether you got anything worth remembering out of it, because from now on it's going to be downhill all the way.'

He turned on his heel, went back to his chair and pulled it close to the table. Then he pushed his face across until he was staring straight into Gregory's face. Gregory held his glance for as long as he could and then his eyes fell and he shuffled uneasily. Barlow leaned back and laughed. He reached in his pocket, took out a packet of cigarettes and lit one.

'Just tricks,' he said.

'What?' Gregory looked startled at the confession.

'I said "Just tricks" . . . Cheap, psychological tricks. To make you uneasy, nervous, frightened. That's all they are . . . They shouldn't worry you. But they do, don't they? You're much more nervous now than you were ten minutes ago. And quite right too.'

Barlow leant forward and his voice took on a caressing note.

'Because, believe me, lad, you've got an awful lot to be nervous about.'

'Such as?'

The attempt at bravado was determined but Gregory's hands

were trembling slightly. Barlow stared at them. Gregory noticed, and hid his hands beneath the table. Barlow smiled sweetly at him.

'Well – for a start – ask yourself why I'm here.'

'I'd prefer to ask you.'

'Very good. Beginning to fight back a little bit. I like that. It makes it more fun . . . All right, I'll tell you. I am here because I want to know all about you and your friends.'

'What makes me and my friends so interesting?'

'Oh no. You've got it wrong.'

Barlow got up and strolled around the table again.

'You're not interesting at all. You're just in the way. There are some other people behind you. They are the ones I find interesting. But first I have to tidy you up, get you out of the way. That's all. You're about as important as a fly.'

Barlow lifted his hand over Gregory's head with the thumb extended and squashed his thumb down on top of his nose. Gregory pulled his head away, tears coming into his eyes.

'Leave me alone.'

'No.' Barlow went back to his chair, took out his packet of cigarettes again. But this time he left them on the table . . . 'No, Gregory. I'm not going to leave you alone until you've told me everything I want to know. You'll nod off to sleep and I'll be sitting here when you wake up. You'll stare at the wall and count the bricks to try and pass the time. But when you look back, I'll still be here. Just asking questions.'

He sat back and lit his cigarette, not taking his eyes off Gregory's face. Gregory sat staring at the table. There was a sudden scrape as Barlow pushed his chair back. He tilted it slightly and crossed his legs. When he spoke again, his voice was conversational.

'What were the guns for?'

Gregory did not answer. Barlow continued to puff gently at his cigarette.

'What were the guns for, Gregory?'

There was no sign that Gregory had even heard.

'What were they for? They must have been for something, mustn't they? Because you paid good money for them. Unless, of course, somebody gave them to you.'

Barlow paused hopefully. From the other side of the table there was silence . . .

'Ah well,' he said. 'I suppose if you don't want to talk to me now, I can't make you.' Gregory looked up. As he did so, Barlow's fist crashed onto the table just in front of his face. The fist moved and grabbed Gregory's collar, pulling him half way across the desk. From three inches away Barlow's voice hissed at him.

'That's what you think, isn't it, Gregory? You think you can win. Well, you can't. They all start off that way. But you can't win. Because it's not fair, this game. Oh, the rules are fair. The rules about charging people and letting them out again. All those rules. But that's all. The rest of it isn't fair at all, Gregory. Because I'm much bigger than you are. You're just a fly. And nobody is ever fair to flies.'

The fist pushed and let go. Gregory fell back in his chair, staring at Barlow, his hands, still trembling, fumbling to straighten his collar. He was obviously expecting another onslaught. But instead, Barlow was staring at him rather oddly. Suddenly Barlow got up and began strolling across towards the door of the cell. But before reaching it he turned and strolled back. Then he came to stand over Gregory again. But this time there was nothing threatening in his manner. In fact, he seemed positively cheerful.

'Have a cigarette.'

In some bewilderment, Gregory took one. Barlow held out a lighter and waited until Gregory had drawn smoke into his lungs.

'You know, humility is a wonderful thing.' Barlow had gone back to his seat and was sitting looking totally relaxed, giving the impression of settling down to an amiable conversation with an old friend.

'I have a genuinely humble streak in me, you know. And I shall always be grateful for it. Because had I not been genuinely humble I might have made a very bad mistake. Because it suddenly occurred to me a moment ago that there's something wrong. From the moment I came in here I realised you were frightened. But I assumed you were frightened of me and what I represent. After all, quite a lot of people are, especially when they have something to hide. And you do. But then I spotted what was wrong.'

He paused and beamed paternally at Gregory, who stared warily back. Gradually the sunny atmosphere in the cell was growing chilly again. Barlow leant forward and stubbed out his cigarette. Then he plucked Gregory's cigarette from between his fingers and stubbed that out as well.

'Don't you want to know what it was, Gregory? ... No? Well, I'll tell you. You're scared. That's one thing. But your sort usually make all kinds of noises to try and get out of situations like these. They ask for lawyers and demand to be charged, shout about their rights and civil liberties and so on. You haven't done any of those things, not even after I deliberately pushed the idea at you a minute or two ago. You're scared of me, all right. But you're even more scared of being let out again, aren't you? Why, Gregory? Who are you scared of?'

Gregory's hands were shaking again. But this time he wasn't even bothering to hide them. Barlow leant across and smiled at him. He went on talking quietly but persistently while Gregory began to shake uncontrollably.

'You are frightened of them, aren't you, Gregory? Well, shall I tell you what I'm going to do? I'm going to let you go. You don't want to tell me anything and you are quite within your rights not to do so. I could press charges, of course. Quite serious ones. Under Section 16 of the Weapons Act 1968 I could do you for possession of firearms without a certificate and with intent to endanger life. I know my law, you see, and I could get you put away for quite a while. But I've decided to let you go instead. So get up, Gregory, and walk out of that door ... Go on ...'

Barlow paused and looked at the man opposite him. Gregory's

eyes were looking back at him but he wasn't seeing Barlow's face. Then his head fell forward into his hands and he began to sob. Barlow pushed back his chair, paused for a moment looking down and then turned on his heel. He walked quickly to the door, opened it, and jerked his head at the constable outside.

'Come in. And bring your notebook. Mr Gregory is going to talk to us after all.'

II

Barlow was at his desk by eight o'clock the next morning. He plugged the telephone through from his secretary's desk to his own. An hour later he had made twenty-five calls, mostly to policemen up and down the country. One had been to a barman at an hotel in Whitechapel, another to a girl who worked for a firm of apparently respectable solicitors. All of them had begun the same way, with a grunted 'This is Barlow here . . .' All of them had ended the same way – with a crisp 'Within twenty-four hours if you can'. Barlow's ear was sore from being held against the receiver. He had broken one pencil in dialling. He got up and went in search of a cup of coffee. For the moment, there was nothing more he could do. It was up to the machine.

It was a good machine. Nothing dramatic would happen. No doors would be kicked in. No cars would come sliding to a halt beside a pavement with rear doors opening and barked commands to 'Get in. The boss wants to see you'. Much of it would consist of policemen calmly hunting through files or consulting sheaves of documents. One or two men would be asking questions – not many, but enough to convey that answers were needed and would be appreciated.

Barlow was banking on one factor above all. The criminal world didn't like its routine disturbed. The knowledge that a hunt was going on was worrying. Even more worrying was the hint which would be dropped where it would reach the ears that mattered – the hint that unless this hunt were successful, an even bigger, more disruptive one might start. Barlow was asking to be bought off – with an offering of his chosen victims. In this case, the victims were outsiders, not part of the criminal world, and with luck the criminal world, for the sake of being left alone to go about its business, would deliver them up.

It was good thinking ... good policeman's thinking. But it didn't work.

At the same desk, twenty-four hours later, Barlow stared at the few scattered pieces of information which were all that had reached him and admitted that this was something new. Nobody was saying anything at all. He reached for Gregory's statement. Despite all the hysteria that had accompanied it, it hadn't told Barlow anything he hadn't been able to guess already. Gregory had been at one of the meetings which Meadows, the criminal, had also attended. The only discussion had been about the possibility of recruiting other members. No names had been mentioned, but Gregory must have looked nervous or worried, because afterwards Meadows had come up to him. Gregory had refused to say what passed between them but he was obviously terrified of Meadows. Quite rightly, thought Barlow, as he read the skimpy document again. Mr Meadows was not a man to take lightly. But otherwise, there was nothing. There were no names that weren't known already, and no indication of what plans, if any, had been made.

Barlow pushed the statement aside and stared grimly at the wall opposite. Fenton's words formed a large bubble in the front of his mind: 'You wanted it. You've got it. So make sure you get it right, won't you?'

He was still sitting there two hours later when the phone rang. It was the commissionaire at reception downstairs.

'Mr Barlow? There is a lady here to see you. She says she

hasn't an appointment but it could be important. Her name is Miss Everrett.'

'Have her brought up.'

He had no idea what Maggie Everrett wanted but at least it would be better than staring at the wall. He opened his outer door and watched the messenger leading her down the corridor towards him. She looked up and saw him and smiled. Barlow found himself thinking that there were times when he wished he wasn't an overweight policeman. This was one of them. He waved her in and she sat opposite him, looking solemn and a trifle uncertain.

'I came to say thank you.'

Barlow waved a dismissive hand and opened his mouth to speak but she interrupted him.

'And don't say all in a day's work, because I know it wasn't. You were kind and very gentle and I'm grateful to you.'

She paused and looked across the desk at him and then burst out laughing. 'Why, Chief Superintendent, you've gone quite pink. If you weren't a policeman I would say you were blushing. How lovely.'

Barlow tried to look stern, failed and grinned instead. He rose majestically to his feet.

'Young lady, you are within Home Office precincts and the one thing people do not do within these hallowed walls is laugh – at least not like that. And certainly not at chief superintendents. It's an offence against the Showing Proper Respect to Senior Policemen Act. Since that is the case I could either arrest you or invite you to lunch. The choice is up to you.'

For a moment she looked doubtful.

'I should go back to the office and do some work. On the other hand' – the smile that Barlow found so enchanting crept back again – 'if you arrested me *and* took me to lunch I would have to come with you, wouldn't I?'

Barlow put an arm around her shoulders.

'Consider yourself arrested,' he said. As they left the office he caught a hastily suppressed look of astonishment on his secretary's face. He winked at her and, with Maggie on his arm, swept out. His secretary stared after them – and the telephone rang. She picked it up.

'Is Barlow there?' said a voice.

'No, I'm afraid he's just left for lunch. Can I take a message?'

'Damn. How long ago?'

'Just a minute ago. Can I take a message?'

'No. I'll get in touch later.'

'Can I say who called?'

'Yes. Tell him it's the man with the chilblains.'

'I beg your pardon?'

'He'll understand . . . Oh Christ!'

There was a thump and the secretary heard a muffled sound of voices. There was a louder noise of something bumping against the receiver. Then silence. She listened, and there was a click as the receiver was put back on the hook. She put the phone down and dialled reception.

'Has Mr Barlow left yet?'

'Yes, miss. He went out just a minute ago.'

'Is he still outside? Can you catch him please and bring him to the phone.'

'I'm sorry, miss. He's gone. There was a taxi just drawn up outside and he and the young lady got straight into it.'

Barlow's secretary put the phone down slowly. The man with the chilblains had had rather a pleasant voice but, just at the end, it hadn't sounded pleasant at all. It had sounded very frightened.

The lunch passed pleasantly. It was only over coffee that Maggie returned to the subject that had brought them together.

'I really am grateful – such a load off my mind.'

Barlow spoke gently: 'And off your bank balance.'

She flushed hard. 'You know how I . . . ?' Her voice trailed away.

'In detail. You've been thieving. In current jargon you have been actively engaged in criminal deception.'

She pursed her mouth. 'At least I've confessed.'

'To?'

'To the people at work, and to you.'

'Not to me. I haven't heard a word.'

'But I'm admitting . . .'

'And I'm deaf.' Barlow paused. 'How did your employers react?'

'They're shocked – and they're thinking it over. With luck they'll settle for getting the money back.'

'And for a consistently detailed scrutiny of your expenses, I hope.'

'That was a rotten thing to say.'

'It was a planned and consistently rotten thing you did. Count yourself lucky'

She smiled wanly. 'I do.'

'Good.' Barlow leant across and poured her another cup of coffee. 'I should hate to have to end our beautiful friendship by locking you up.'

She looked up at him.

'I suppose this is the end though, isn't it? After all, it's finished and done with now . . . Except, there is one thing. I don't know whether it matters but I thought I would tell you about it. Of course, it may not be important at all.'

'Tell me.'

'Well, I was talking to a colleague of mine and he mentioned that he'd been looking into some of these protest groups again. He went to some party last night and he heard a couple of rather nasty specimens talking out in the passageway. He didn't know what they were talking about but he did catch a couple of phrases. One of them said something about, "It will make headlines all over the world", and the other said, "It's the one thing everybody's scared of" . . . .'

'Who were they? Did he know?'

'No. He hadn't seen them before, but he said that the others at the party were very respectful towards them, even seemed a bit in awe of them. He got the impression they were bigger fish than the others. They didn't really talk to anyone else and they both left separately soon afterwards. John was just interested because they were such odd sentences. He and I were trying to think what on earth they could have been talking about . . . But it could be nothing at all.'

'It could be,' Barlow said thoughtfully. 'It isn't exactly what you would call evidence. But in this particular case we haven't got much of that anyway. Where can I find this friend of yours?'

'I share an office with him. His name's John Dyson. You could come back with me now, if you like.'

Barlow thought for a moment.

'I should really go back to my office . . . No.' He got to his feet and signalled the waiter. 'Let's go and see your friend. If I'm going to get nowhere I might as well do it that way as any other. Beside,' he grinned at her, 'I'm still involved in this television liaison job, remember? It's time I started to liaise on a slightly broader basis, otherwise people will start to talk.'

'Why, Mr Barlow,' Maggie said, dropping a mock curtsey, 'If you weren't such a very important policeman I should say you were making a pass at me.'

'Policemen don't make passes,' said Barlow as he held the door open for her.

'I'm so glad. After all, harm can come to a young girl like that . . . can't it?'

Barlow followed her out of the restaurant.

'That was a pretty cryptic remark.'

'Yes it was, wasn't it? Why don't you get us a taxi. I'm a great believer in taking everything in stages.'

'So am I,' said Barlow. 'And, apart from anything else, there's the little matter of whatever it is that not only frightens everyone but makes headlines all over the world.'

'Yes,' she said, suddenly solemn. 'You'd better come and talk to John Dyson and see if he can help.'

12

It was five o'clock by the time Barlow lumbered out of another taxi outside the Home Office. As he climbed the stairs to his office, he reflected gloomily that apart from a staleness after drinking wine at lunch he wasn't much further forward. Maggie's colleague, Dyson, had been dubious at first about talking to him, but between them he and Maggie had persuaded him that he wasn't committing a breach of professional ethics or running any risk of damaging his own personal contacts. He had had only one piece of information to add. As he had been going up the stairs to the party which was being held in a flat on the top floor, one of the men he had overheard had been using the pay telephone in the hall. Barlow fished in his pocket for the note he had taken of Dyson's precise words:

'He was talking a foreign language. It wasn't any language I know, certainly not German or French or Italian or Spanish. It didn't sound Scandinavian either. In fact, it didn't sound like any language I'd ever heard before . . . No, I don't know any Russian. But when he was talking upstairs later, he didn't have any trace of a foreign accent. He was speaking standard BBC-type English.'

Barlow was still staring at his notes as he pushed open the door of his office. His secretary jumped up from behind her desk.

Barlow looked up, saw her face and shut the door quickly behind him.

'All right,' he said. 'Tell me.'

After hearing about the call, he thought for a moment and then picked up the phone. He dialled quickly, then put his hand over the phone:

'Get me Mr Fenton on the other line.'

As it happened, Fenton came through first. Barlow told him rapidly what had happened and then said, 'Hold on a moment' . . . He spoke rapidly into the other phone.

'Ted? It's Charlie Barlow here. Listen, I want a car and I want one of your fellows who knows Meadows and knows his patch. I want him outside here in an hour and I want him all night . . . What? . . . No, I won't cross any wires. I just want to be sure that if I have to talk to Meadows I'll know where to find him . . . No, I won't do anything stupid. I just want to have a little chat with him, that's all . . . Right. Thanks.'

He slammed the receiver down and turned back to Fenton's call.

'Sorry, sir . . . Yes . . . Yes, I think that's a good idea. I'll be along right away.'

Fenton was on the phone when Barlow entered and he looked like a man who was hearing bad news. He motioned Barlow to a chair and went on listening.

'All right,' he said finally. 'I'll pass that on . . . You'll keep us posted? . . . Thank you.'

He put the phone down and walked across to the office cabinet. Reaching into it, he produced a bottle of whisky and two glasses. Barlow felt a chill creeping over him. If Fenton thought the occasion warranted whisky, then the news must be very bad indeed. He poured two glasses and handed one to Barlow.

'They've found our friend,' he said abruptly. 'He was dumped on a building site in Hackney.'

Barlow looked a question.

'No, he's not dead. But, according to the doctor who examined him, he has been systematically and brutally beaten. He may lose the sight of one eye and he has several fractures of both arms. He's unconscious but apparently he did come round at one stage. According to the doctor he muttered, "Harlow", which I take to mean you . . . Then he said, "looking for an axeman". Or, at least, that's what they thought he said. Does that convey anything to you?'

'An axeman?' Barlow sounded almost indignant. 'The only thing "axeman" means to me is that Mitchell fellow. But he's dead.'

'Well according to the doctor that is what he heard. But he said our friend wasn't talking very clearly. In fact, he said he was surprised he was talking at all.'

'Yes.' Barlow finished his drink. 'We'll do something about that. I shall try and do something about that this evening.'

Fenton nodded Barlow towards the whisky bottle.

'What did you have in mind?'

'I thought I would go and have a chat with our Mr Meadows.'

'Is that wise? Aren't you likely to do no more than show him that we are suspicious.'

'I don't know.' Barlow got up and began to prowl around the office with the air of a man who was looking for something to kick.

'But we certainly aren't getting anywhere just sitting here.'

'Axeman.' Fenton picked up a Biro and wrote it in block capitals on the pad in front of him. 'Does this man Meadows have any colleagues who go by that name? Anyone he uses for violent work?'

'If he does it's news to me. And I would know.' Barlow started on another prowling circuit of the office. Suddenly he stopped dead.

'Wait a minute. You said he wasn't talking very clearly?'

'That is what the doctor said. Apparently, the gentlemen who dealt with our friend had also broken his jaw.'

Barlow leant over Fenton's desk and spun Fenton's pad towards him. The word 'axeman' stared up at him.

'That isn't what he said. What did he say? The whole thing.'

Fenton consulted his notes. 'The doctor says that what he heard sounded like "looking for an axeman". He wasn't too sure about the "looking" even.'

'Precisely. If your jaw's been broken you can't say consonants clearly. He wasn't saying "axeman" at all. What he was trying to say was "cracksman". They're looking for a cracksman.'

Fenton stared dubiously at his pad.

'I suppose that makes slightly more sense. But why? Why should they be looking for a cracksman. Why "looking"? Meadows and his confederates would presumably know where to find one without any difficulty at all?'

'I'll tell you exactly why.'

Barlow flopped back into his chair with an air of triumph.

'Because they had one. They had Charlie Billings.'

'And who is Charlie Billings?'

'Charlie Billings is a cracksman ... one of the best in the business.'

'So if they had Charlie Billings as you say,' Fenton was veering between distaste at the conversation and impatience at its lack of development ... 'If they had this man Billings why should they be looking for someone else?'

'Because yesterday evening, acting on a tip-off about some stolen jewellery, the Yard arrested Charlie Billings. He's been charged with receiving. He was up in court this morning. Bail was refused. Charlie's under lock and key. He's no good to them any more, so they're looking for another one. And they obviously need him urgently.'

'Yes, I think it's safe to assume they do.'

None of Barlow's exhuberance was rubbing off on Fenton. He pushed the whisky bottle towards Barlow again.

'Help yourself to a stiff one, Charles. You're going to need it. Because our friend did say something else before he lost consciousness again.'

Fenton paused for effect.

'This time, according to the doctor, it was fairly clear. He said'

... Fenton paused and looked down at his notes again.

'He said, "Only two days to go".'

They stared at each other in silence. Fenton opened his mouth to speak but the phone rang. He picked it up, listened for a moment and then passed the receiver to Barlow.

'Yes?' Barlow barked into the phone.

'Ease up, Charlie,' said the voice at the other end. 'You nearly took my ear off.' Barlow put a hand over the mouthpiece.

'It's Ted Matthews from the Yard. He was putting me onto Meadows.'

He went back to the phone.

'Sorry Ted ... What is it?'

'It's Meadows,' said the voice at the other end. 'I thought before giving you one of our lads I'd get him to do a little checking – just to save time. He's with me now. It appears Meadows has vanished. He was around last night – down at that club of his. He left there late, said he might be away for a few days and then cleared off this morning. Nobody seems to know where. Or if they do, they aren't telling. He's nowhere near that house he has outside Oxford, but we don't think he's left the country because our friends usually let us know if he does that. So it's anybody's guess where he is.'

Barlow thought for a moment.

'That lad of yours, Ted – is he good?'

'One of the best.'

'Could I borrow him for a bit?'

'How long would you want him?'

'I'm not sure. But it wouldn't be more than two days. It can't be more than two days.' There was a pause at the other end.

'It's like that, is it? All right, Charlie. You can have him. I'll put him onto you now. And Charlie?'

'Yes?'

'Anything else – just ask.'

A second voice came on the phone, younger and rather cautious, obviously not certain what it was getting itself into.

'Yes sir? . . .'

'What's your name, son?'

'DC Edwards, sir. Glyn Edwards.'

'Welsh?'

'Liverpool Welsh sir.'

'Nice combination.'

'Thank you, sir. I'll try not to disappoint you.'

'You'd better not. Now listen and listen hard. You are going to find a cracksman. I want one. I want to know the best four men available now, at this moment, free to do a job in the next two days. Report to me here in person in half an hour – with a car. Then we'll go and have a chat with them.'

'Yes, sir . . . Excuse my asking, sir. But you haven't changed sides, have you?'

'Don't make jokes. There isn't time.'

Barlow thumped the receiver back in its rest and looked at Fenton.

'It's a lead,' he said.

'I agree,' said Fenton. 'It does appear to be the only slender thread of information we have, apart from the knowledge that it has to lead us to the right place in rather less than forty-eight hours . . . whatever that place is.'

Barlow nodded but in a vague, preoccupied way.

'Headlines all over the world,' he murmured to himself.

'What was that?'

'I'm sorry, sir.' Rapidly Barlow told Fenton about the conversation he had had with Maggie's colleague . . .

Even Fenton's normal imperturbality was a trifle shaken. 'It certainly leaves room for guesswork, doesn't it?'

He drew a piece of paper towards him and started to doodle on it, jotting names as he went along . . . 'The Queen . . . or Prince Philip . . . or any of the children. Where's Charles at the moment? . . . Prime Minister . . . probably not any of the Cabinet. The prospect of losing merely the odd Cabinet Minister isn't frightening enough . . .'

'It doesn't have to be just an assassination attempt against one individual,' said Barlow. 'A nice big bomb and you could kill quite a few. And some of this lot are quite keen on bombs.'

Fenton looked up, nodded grimly and added to his list . . . 'Buckingham Palace, Ten Downing Street . . . and, I suppose, the House of Commons. This lot seem to be better organised than Guy Fawkes.'

'Wait a minute. We have got more to go on than that. There's the cracksman. Don't forget him.'

'If that is what our friend was saying. It's only a piece of guesswork on your part, Charles, although I agree a perfectly reasonable one. That would seem to imply something or someone protected by elaborate keys within a particular area. The Prime Minister in Downing Street rather than the whole House of Commons at a sitting.'

'Or something . . .' Barlow stroked his chin . . . 'The Bank of England, do you think . . .?' 'It's possible.' Fenton was now drawing nervous, stabbing doodles of bombs with curly fuses. 'Except there is that phrase, "It's the one thing everybody's scared of" . . . I would take that to mean something like an assassination attempt on royalty or the Prime Minister. The sort of thing we have all been frightened of ever since Kennedy.'

'Yes, that's true. But there is one other thing.' Barlow had been leafing back through his notes. Fenton drew a much bigger bomb and viciously wrote 'bomb' in the middle.

'There are a great many other things, Charles.'

He put his pen down and got to his feet.

'I'm sorry. I didn't mean to sound irritable. Let's have it.'

'It's the involvement of Meadows. We've been thinking in terms of a political gesture – assassination or an act of terror, working on the basis of these people's desire to disrupt the country just for the sake of doing so. But Meadows is a businessman. He's in it for the money. He wouldn't become involved in any project unless there were a considerable profit somewhere along the line.'

Fenton sat down again rather abruptly.

'So where does that leave us? . . . Ruling out assassination, you think? Well, at least, that's some kind of relief.'

'Not really, sir.'

It was Barlow's turn to betray the tension by getting up and moving uneasily about the room. He walked over to the bookcase and stood there staring at it. 'It sounds a wild idea but we're dealing with a wild bunch . . . It's just this phrase popped into my head . . . a king's ransom.'

'Or a queen's.' Fenton added the unnecessary words very slowly. He pushed back his chair and went over to the window. It was growing dark and in the street below the office workers and civil servants were crowding along the streets. Across the road lights still burned and the cars and buses were beginning to settle into their jerky rush-hour procession. Fenton drummed uneasily on the window pane. Then he swung on his heel.

'What if we asked every single person we know to be even vaguely connected with this enterprise to accompany a police officer to a station and questioned every single one of them. Could we get results that way?'

Barlow shook his head. 'I thought of that. But we haven't got time. The little fish wouldn't know anything. They would be like Gregory. The big ones wouldn't say anything. We would have no grounds for holding them, even assuming we could find them, that is. Don't forget that Meadows has vanished. And without a charge – and time – I couldn't guarantee anything.'

'Yes.' Fenton gave the window an irritable knock. 'It's at moments like this that one wishes one had the freedom of action of some other police forces one could mention.'

Even Barlow blinked slightly at this. But before he could say anything, Fenton clicked his fingers.

'I've got it. The cracksman. How many really top-flight cracksmen would you say there are in this country?'

'About six,' said Barlow. 'And I know what you're going to suggest . . . That we pull all of them in.'

'Why not, man? They need one. If they haven't got one, they can't go ahead.'

'But we can't be sure of that.'

The two of them were facing each other across the desk, both gripping its sides.

'Yes, we can. We'd be depriving them of an essential part of their plan.'

'But we don't know what that plan is. We know they need a cracksman. But we don't know that he is absolutely essential. Or that he *has* to be of the really top flight. They might be able to go ahead with just an ordinary second-rate man. There are a hundred of those.'

'No. That's not how I would read that message. It was important. If he were trying that hard to tell us, then he obviously thought it was the key.'

'All right. But there's another reason it won't work.'

'What's that?'

'Meadows. Meadows is big. If we knocked off every single top cracksman in this country, Meadows is perfectly capable of getting one from abroad and having him here within twelve hours. We might make it more difficult for him. But we can't guarantee that we shall have stopped him. And we still shan't know what it is we're trying to stop.'

Slowly Fenton eased himself away from the desk, uncurling his fingers and straightening his back. Barlow did the same and then looked irritably at his watch.

'Where the hell's Edwards? He should be here by now!'

Suddenly he froze, staring down at his watch, then gradually lifted his head. Fenton was looking at him in alarm.

'Are you all right, Charles?'

He moved towards him, stretching out a hand, but was pushed aside as Barlow jumped for the phone. He dialled frantically, then stood over the phone, muttering at it through clenched teeth.

'Come on, damn you ... Come on ... Hallo? .. Miss Margaret Everrett please ... Hallo? ... She's where? Then can you transfer me, please. Thank you ...'

There was a pause while Fenton thoughtfully looked on, absentmindedly rubbing the shoulder which Barlow had bumped on his way round the desk.

'Hallo? Maggie. This is Barlow. Listen. It's very important. Where's that fellow, Dyson? The one who heard the men talking . . . He is? Put him on . . . Mr Dyson. Listen. This is extremely urgent. Can you stay where you are for another ten minutes? Give me the extension number. Right. In a few minutes a man is going to ring you and say something to you. I just want you to listen. Then I shall phone you again. All right? Fine.'

Fenton started to speak but Barlow's hand flapped him into silence. Then he began to dial again. But this time a longer string of digits. The phone was answered almost at once and Barlow wasted no time on preliminaries.

'Price, I want some help. Get a pencil and take this number down . . .'

Barlow rattled off a string of instructions while Fenton listened at first with bewilderment and then with growing interest. Barlow put the phone down and began to prowl about the room, muttering to himself . . .

'Right . . . Thirty seconds to dial and get through . . . That's it. Should be through by now. Talk to Dyson . . . That's it.'

He grabbed the phone, dialled, and gave an extension number.

'Hallo? What? It's engaged? . . . I'll hold on please. And put me through as soon as the caller clears. It's very urgent.'

There was a pause while Barlow avoided looking at Fenton. Then he spoke again. 'Hallo? Mr Dyson? Well? . . .'

Fenton heard a voice at the other end, speaking quickly and, it seemed to him, affirmatively. Barlow cut in.

'You're sure? A lot could depend on it . . . Right. Thank you very much.'

He put the phone down and turned to Fenton.

'The man who spoke to Dyson was talking the same language as those two men he overheard. It was George Price – a DI in Pontrhyd – and he was talking Welsh.'

'Welsh . . .' Fenton repeated thoughtfully. 'It's an interesting piece of information but I'm not sure it gets us anywhere.'

Barlow picked up the phone and began to dial.

'That fellow should have turned up at reception by now. Hallo? Barlow here. I'm expecting a DC Edwards . . . Not yet? All right. Let me know as soon as he turns up.'

He put the phone down and turned back to Fenton.

'I think it does get us somewhere. I think that if there are Welshmen involved, it means that whatever is going to happen is likely to be happening in Wales. The Welsh don't go in for violence much and all their demonstrations are fairly small scale. They aren't like the Irish. If you weren't planning an operation in Wales, there wouldn't be any reason for including Welshmen in it.'

Fenton still looked vaguely unconvinced.

'I suppose that's a point. Still where in Wales? It may be a small country but it isn't that small. It also doesn't include that many targets one would have thought dramatic enough for this exercise . . . Although – wait a minute . . . the Royal Mint is there now, isn't it? That would qualify surely? Charles? . . .'

He leant across and shook Barlow by the arm – justifiably, since Barlow patently wasn't listening. Instead he was staring at a copy of the *Daily Telegraph* which lay on the desk in front of him. Without a word, he picked it up, folded it across and passed it to Fenton, his thumb pointing at the relevant paragraph. Fenton took it. It was an article about industrial development in the Midlands. But it began with a discussion of water supplies. The opening sentence ran:

'In two days' time the Queen will declare open the new reservoir in Wales which is the latest in the chain supplying water to the Midlands.'

Fenton slowly lowered the paper onto the desk and looked at Barlow. Neither of them said anything for a moment. Fenton straightened the blotting paper on his desk with both hands.

'It would appear to meet the criteria, Charles. Our Welsh friends are notoriously sensitive about their drowned valleys, and the blowing up of Her Majesty while she is declaring one open would certainly make headlines all round the world.'

Barlow spoke slowly and carefully, thinking it out as he went along.

'They would need a cracksman to lay the charges – in the pumphouse or somewhere.'

'What about the involvement of your criminal friend?'

Barlow paused for a moment: 'Yes. He doesn't really fit. Unless . . . If they did commit this outrage there would be chaos. Every policeman and task force for miles around would be pulled in. Ideal conditions for criminals to operate elsewhere.'

'I see.' Fenton's fingers drummed uneasily on the desk. 'Meadows finances the operation as a gigantic diversionary exercise for several other schemes of his own. Yes – that could make sense.'

Both men stared at each other in silence. Suddenly the phone rang. Barlow picked it up.

'Yes? All right. No. I'm coming down.'

He put the receiver slowly back on the rest and looked across at Fenton. 'That was Edwards. He will have a short-list of possible cracksmen who might be involved. Shall I pursue that line? Or would you prefer me to be available here?'

Fenton shook himself slightly, like a man trying to get rid of the last few moments of a bad dream. He squared his shoulders.

'No, Charles. You pursue that line of inquiry. But I should like you here by 9.30 this evening, please. To report.'

'Right.'

Barlow got up. He was at the door when Fenton spoke again.

'And Charles?'

'Yes, sir.'

'That report will not just be to me. There will be others present.'

Barlow nodded his understanding. As he left, Fenton picked up the red phone. And even before the door closed, Barlow heard his voice.

'This is Fenton. I need to see the Minister, urgently.'

PART III

13

When Barlow reached reception, Detective Constable Edwards was waiting by the door. He was eager, bright-eyed, and surprisingly short.

'You another Nipper?' asked Barlow.

Edwards grinned. 'Shan't complain if I get as far as Nipper Reed, sir. And, like him, I did have to do a bit of standing on my toes to qualify.'

'So long as you keep off mine,' said Barlow. He gave a jerk of the head and Edwards followed him outside. On the pavement he anticipated Barlow's query by indicating an MG sports car parked a few yards up the street. The two men climbed into it, Barlow inserting himself with some difficulty. Once the operation had been completed, Edwards, who had been staring tactfully out of the window, turned his head, and handed Barlow a sheet of paper.

'I thought we might start with Danny Reynolds, sir. He's one of the best and we're fairly sure of finding him at home.'

Barlow nodded agreement and the car headed south towards Battersea Bridge. The list was short: five names and a few brief notes on each. Barlow had only met one of the men but he knew all the names. Between them, they represented the élite of an élite profession, although outside their own small, secretive world they were totally unknown. But if Meadows were recruiting a first-class cracksman, his name had to be on this list. Barlow checked again. One of the men was in hospital. Of the four others, one was believed to be involved in the planning of a bank robbery due to take place sometime in the next ten days. Another was thought to have been involved in the theft of a considerable amount of jewellery from a flat in Knightsbridge a few days earlier. It would be unusual for him to undertake another job so soon The two other names had no information against them.

Barlow looked up. They had crossed the river and were working their way up the back streets of Battersea towards Clapham Common. Barlow checked Reynolds' address. He lived in one of the houses just behind the Common, a quiet, respectable area, currently going up in the social scale. Most of the people living there would have bought their houses in the last five or six years, painted them white, knocked down interior walls and fitted roller blinds rather than curtains in the windows. The car drew up. Reynolds' house still had curtains.

As he waited in the car, while Edwards went up to the front door, Barlow looked around at the other houses and considered idly how surprised any of their occupants would have been to discover that their neighbour was one of the ablest criminals in London. They would have been given no clues. Reynolds would have taken enormous care to appear as a rather dull, ordinary citizen, inclined to keep himself to himself, and totally lacking in interest in anyone but himself. No flashy American cars would draw up here or men in dark glasses swagger to the door. Just, occasionally, Mr Reynolds would be away for a couple of days – 'on business'. Once, Barlow remembered, he had been away for a couple of years. But that was all. Reynolds, as behoved a skilled craftsman, was a very careful man.

Edwards was talking to someone at the front door, although Barlow couldn't see who. He had a vague memory of there having been something slightly odd in Reynolds' background – something about his family. He was just trying to track down the memory when Edwards reappeared at the car window.

'Reynolds is walking the dog on the Common, sir. We can drive part of the way.'

A few seconds later Barlow grunted and painfully squeezed himself out of the car. Together he and Edwards walked onto the footpath that led across the middle of the Common. Circling around it doggedly were a handful of dog-walkers engaged in their evening ritual. Through the dusk Barlow saw a man standing staring towards them while a black Labrador chased the ball he had just thrown for it. He was slightly built, spectacled, and had a cloth cap jammed hard down almost over his ears. The figure was quite still but gave an impression of alertness. It didn't need Edwards's quiet 'That's Reynolds' to tell Barlow that this was their man and that he had recognized them for what they were.

As they came alongside, Reynolds nodded a greeting:

'Evening, Mr Edwards.'

'Good evening . . . This is Mr Barlow.'

'Evening.'

He gave no indication that the name meant anything to him, though Barlow was fairly sure that the details of his career were as well known to Reynolds as Reynolds' activities were to him. The three of them stood in silence for a moment before Edwards made the first move.

'Mr Barlow was hoping you might be able to help us, Mr Reynolds. It's rather important.'

Barlow cleared his throat.

'It's more than that. It's very important.' He turned to Edwards. 'I'll see you back in the car.'

Edwards was too well trained to look disconcerted, but from his flicker of hesitation it was obvious he hadn't expected to be dismissed quite so summarily. Still he turned on his heel and walked away without a word. Barlow and Reynolds began to stroll along the footpath. The dog returned with the ball. Reynolds bent down and threw it again.

'It must be very important to bring you out, Mr Barlow.'

There was the faintest stress on the pronoun.

'It is. I want help and I want information.'

Reynolds turned his head to look at Barlow for a moment.

'I knew you wanted something . . . but information?'

'I know you're not a grass. This *is* out of the ordinary.'

The dog reappeared again, but this time it was Barlow who bent down, picked up the ball and threw it. The ball went further than he had intended and landed in the pond which formed the central meeting place of the Common. The dog looked mildly reproachful for a moment as if to imply that this wasn't the ideal evening for a swim but then bounded away in pursuit.

Barlow walked on a pace or two, then stopped and turned to face Reynolds:

'We know there is an outrage – and I use that word deliberately – planned within the very near future. We know it may take place in Wales. We know it will be designed to do enormous harm to this country. We know various political hooligans are involved. And that's all we know. Except that it involves the services of a cracksman.'

Reynolds was looking away from Barlow, across the common.

'I'm moving a few feet away from you now.'

He caught the look of bewilderment on Barlow's face and allowed a very faint smile to appear on his own.

'Nothing personal. My dog's on his way back, and since you sent him into the pond I don't see why you shouldn't suffer the consequences.'

Barlow turned around fractionally too late to avoid a shower of spray as the Labrador skidded to a halt, dumped the ball at Barlow's feet and then shook itself violently. Reynolds waited until the performance was over, before drifting back. He picked the ball up, put it in his pocket and clicked his fingers at the dog which fell in obediently behind them as they walked on.

'Your word was "outrage". Now one man's outrage might be another man's political gesture. In either case, I can't help you.'

'You can't or won't?'

'I've always had two or three simple rules. One: never get

involved except in your own business. This is not my business.'

'It may not be your business but I think you know about it. I think you were offered it, and that you turned it down. I also suspect you know who took it on in your place.'

They reached the edge of the pond. Reynolds paused for a moment, watching a couple of fishermen still attempting to trap one of the few tired fish that survived in the stagnant, oily water. Then he turned and began walking back the way they had come. Barlow returned to the attack.

'We aren't talking about crime. Not what you and I mean by crime. This is political and it's meant to harm this country. It could damage it seriously – possibly beyond repair.'

Reynolds paused and turned to look at Barlow, thoughtfully as if he was considering very carefully. Barlow held his breath.

'You may be right, Mr Barlow. But then I'm not as concerned with politics as you are. I have my own views, of course, but I don't believe in getting involved.'

He strolled on and Barlow watched him go. He decided to have one last attempt, and hurried his pace. He caught up with Reynolds just as he reached the edge of the Common alongside the main road.

'What if I told you that we have very good grounds for believing that an attempt on the life of the Queen is involved?'

Reynolds turned his head and stared at Barlow. But Barlow got the impression that he was puzzled by what he had just heard rather than shocked or surprised.

'Interesting, Mr Barlow, but I've only got your word for it. Still, if it's true you'll be taking precautions. And now it's my tea-time. My wife will have it waiting for me. We like to keep to a regular routine. Good evening, Mr Barlow. Give my regards to Mr Edwards.'

He crossed the road, the Labrador padding obediently at his heels. Danny Reynolds, quiet, pedantic of speech, suburban householder, wouldn't say boo to a goose, 'that nice Mr Reynolds from number 14, such a gentleman . . .' Danny Reynolds who, if the stories were true, had once blown the door off a fairly sizeable safe while he sat on top of it – reading.

Barlow turned on his heel and headed back to the car. A slightly stiff DC Edwards greeted him.

'Any luck, sir?'

'Not a thing. Reynolds knows something. I don't think he's doing the job, but he knows about it. But he wouldn't tell me a thing.'

'I didn't think he would, sir. Danny Reynolds is a great one for minding his own business. When he isn't working I sometimes think he even forgets what his real job is.'

Barlow grunted a reply. He felt he had had enough of Danny Reynolds for one evening. DC Edwards, however, was obviously feeling in a conversational mood. 'I thought we'd try Ryan next, sir. He'll be at the boys' club he helps with, which isn't all that far from here. I don't know whether we'll get any more out of him than we did out of Reynolds, but at least he's a bit chattier.' He slid the MG round the roundabout alongside the entrance to Battersea Fun Fair and headed it down towards Vauxhall. A few minutes later they pulled up outside a Catholic church.

'The club is in the hall round the back, sir' said Edwards. He made no effort to get out of the car but sat watching Barlow walk grimly up the path. Ten minutes later he was walking back down it and Edwards had no need to ask whether he had had any luck. Instead he moved the car off and headed for their next address which lay across the river in Islington.

Two hours and three calls later it was two very silent men who drove back towards the centre of London again – this time from the direction of Golder's Green. Eventually Edwards broke the silence:

'They must be the tightest bunch in the business', he said reflectively. 'You know, the only time that I ever saw Danny worked up about anything was when there was that Smithfield porters' march against the Uganda Asians. I happened to meet him in a pub that night, which is odd in itself because Danny hardly ever has a drink, but he'd had a couple that night and he was shouting the odds all over the place.'

'That's funny,' Barlow was barely interested and sounded it. 'I wouldn't have put Reynolds down as a racialist.'

'Oh no', Edwards spun the wheel to avoid a taxi which had decided to cut across in front of them, 'he isn't. Just the opposite. It's the one thing he can't stand. He's married to a coloured girl. Not an immigrant. Her family have been over here for years. So he's very strong on race prejudice, Danny is. I think their kids get a bit of a rough deal sometimes. . . . Look out, sir, you'll have us on the pavement.'

DC Edwards's alarm was understandable. A few seconds earlier Barlow had been sunk in his seat, staring grimly ahead and barely listening. Now he had suddenly reared up and grabbed Edwards by the arm.

'That's it. I knew there was something. All the time I was talking to him, I knew there was something. The office, quick as you can – and then Clapham Common.

'I want to talk to Reynolds again. But first I have to pick something up at the office. Something that may interest Reynolds very much. Come on. Move.'

With the air of one who was fully aware that his was not to reason why, DC Edwards moved. In fact, he moved to such good effect that the MG skidded to a halt outside the Home Office ten minutes later. Barlow emerged from it like an elephant from a barrel and with a shout of 'Stay there' disappeared through the main doors. In a few minutes he was back, clutching an envelope.

'Back to Danny Reynolds, sir?' said Edwards as the car moved off again.

'Back to Danny Reynolds. But this time we may get results. This time I may have the key to unlock his clam-like soul.'

A few yards further along the corridor from Barlow's office the light still shone beneath Fenton's door. Behind it Fenton picked up the phone for what he estimated would be his thirtieth call since Barlow had left. He dialled a combination of numbers not listed in the public directory, asked for an extension and gave his name. Eventually he was put through. The conversation was brief and to the point:

'You'll have been told what it's all about? . . . I feel your people should be there . . . Good. Yes, I know it's a somewhat unorthodox hour. However we find ourselves in somewhat unorthodox circumstances.'

Fenton replaced the receiver and ticked another name on the list in front of him. Military Intelligence had been last on the list. There would be seven men round the table, and whatever was decided, they would, between them, be able to pick up a phone and order any and every military and police action that might be thought necessary. Fenton got to his feet and stretched. The image of a large brandy to be drunk as he slumped in a large leather armchair had just formed itself in his mind when his phone rang again. Wearily he picked it up:

'Fenton.'

'Good evening, Fenton', said a voice he knew well.

'Good evening.'

'You'll remember one of my fellows who was working with you and got rather badly beaten up?'

'I do indeed. I gather he's going to be all right?'

'Yes. Eventually. We've had someone sitting with him and he came round about half an hour ago. He couldn't tell us much more but I thought you'd like to hear the little we did get.'

'I would indeed. And so would Barlow.'

'Well, it's all a bit disjointed. But as far as we can gather he was eavesdropping somewhere. He couldn't see faces and he didn't recognise voices. But from what he overheard they were discussing two points. One was that they needed a good cracksman.'

'Yes. We worked that one out from what he said earlier.'

'Oh you did? . . . Well, this may not be news to you either then. But whatever our friends are up to involves a ransom of some kind. I don't know what for. But the argument seemed to be about whether they should ask for one million pounds or two and how they were going to collect.'

'A million pounds?'

'That's right. Or two. Interesting, isn't it? It's a little like one of those magazine games to test your social attitudes. What in this country would you give two million pounds to save? We're staying with him round the clock but I don't think he's got any more to tell us. Good luck.'

The phone clicked off, leaving Fenton still staring blankly at the opposite wall. 'What is worth two million pounds to save? What isn't?' he muttered into the dead phone. 'But what is so big that that's the kind of figure you argue about? What – or who? . . . But assassinating the Queen is one thing, kidnapping her is quite another. Or is it? There's always a first time.'

He picked up the phone again.

'Fenton here. Chief Superintendent Barlow is somewhere in London in the company of a Detective Constable Edwards of the Flying Squad. Pass a message to him, please, asking him to ring me. I'll wait here for the answer. Thank you.'

The phone rang again in less than a minute, but by then Fenton's normally impeccable blotting pad was covered with doodles in which millions of pounds figured prominently. He reached for the receiver.

'Yes?'

It was a Scotland Yard operations room inspector who answered him. 'I'm sorry, sir. But Detective Constable Edwards is not in one of our vehicles. He's driving his own car and he isn't in radio contact. If he does contact us, shall we ask him to call you?'

'No thank you.'

'Very good, sir.'

Fenton got up and moved towards the door rapidly before the phone could ring again. He had done all that could be done for the moment. Now it was up to Barlow and, if he failed, to the gentlemen whose evening he had ruined and who were due to assemble very soon. Meanwhile, thought Fenton, he might possibly have two large brandies. It looked as if it was going to be a long night.

Reynolds himself answered the door to Barlow's knock. Predictably, he gave no sign that the return visit was in any way unexpected. Barlow might have been an old friend who always dropped in of an evening. He led Barlow into a room full of startlingly elegant furniture. Barlow's appreciation must have shown on his face, because Reynolds said as he indicated a chair: 'Yes, it is a pleasant room, isn't it? My wife has a knack of acquiring furniture which I think is junk and turns out to be just what the house needs. Do sit down.'

Barlow did so and then took the envelope from his pocket and laid it on the arm of the chair. He saw Reynolds' eyes flick towards it and away again but neither of them made any comment. They sat in silence for a minute or so until Reynolds leant forward:

'May I offer you some refreshment?'

'No thank you,' said Barlow. He nodded at a silver tray near Reynolds' chair. The bottles standing on it included an extremely good malt whisky.

'I'm here uninvited and not very welcome. If I can persuade you that I was right to come back to talk to you, then I'll take a glass of that.'

Reynolds allowed a very small smile to flit across his face. 'You can have a glass now without any conditions.'

'No,' said Barlow briskly, sitting forward suddenly. 'Let's not pretend this is a social occasion. This is business. You are on one side of the law. I'm on the other. We may possibly feel we understand one another more than ordinary members of the public do. But that doesn't alter the fact that, formally speaking, we're on opposite sides. I want to persuade you to join my side for a few minutes. Because I think that in this particular instance you belong on my side.'

'I'd need a lot of convincing.'

'I intend to try.'

Barlow took the envelope from the arm of the chair and held it in front of him with the open flap towards Reynolds.

'I told you earlier what it was all about. I also said that I thought you knew anyway. I am only going to add a couple more facts, which you may not know. The purpose of this enterprise is to make money for some people involved. But it is also to disrupt and damage this country to gain political advantage for some others. Most of those others are revolutionaries . . . Maoists, Trotskyists – call them what you like.'

Reynolds held up a hand and Barlow paused, looking at him keenly.

'I suggest you take a glass of my whisky and we talk of something else. I have political views certainly. But I am not so committed to one extreme or another that I would involve myself for or against any project for that reason.'

'I haven't finished yet.'

Reynolds lowered his hand and settled back in his chair.

'I said that most of the people involved were revolutionaries on the left. But there is one other man closely involved. If this thing goes through, he will get more power somehow. I'm not sure how. I admit that. But he is shrewd enough not to be involved unless he can see some benefit for himself and the views he holds. I suspect he may be encouraging the left-wingers in the hope that if they are successful, there will be a backlash against them – and he will reap the benefit.'

Reynolds was still leaning back in his chair but Barlow sensed that he was listening slightly more closely than he had been.

'Why should I get involved?'

'I haven't told you the name of the politican yet – or what his special fanaticism is. Here is a picture of him talking to other men involved in this scheme. It was Meadows who talked to you. Here is another picture of the group that includes Meadows.'

Barlow leant forward and handed Reynolds the photographs which the man with the chilblains had produced in Fenton's office that day. He sat hardly daring to breathe while Reynolds, his face expressionless, examined them. Finally Reynolds looked up. 'I recognise the – um – "politician". And I know what filth he preaches.'

'Well?'

'These pictures could have been taken any time, anywhere.'

'The man who took them thought they were very important. So did others. So important that three days later they worked him over so badly that he nearly died. He is still in hospital.

Reynolds said nothing. Instead he replaced the photographs in their envelope and handed it back to Barlow. Then quietly he got up and moved over to the door. As he opened it, Barlow tried his last throw.

'How would your wife feel if she knew you were helping that man to power?'

Reynolds turned at the door, his face carefully without expression, looked at Barlow for a moment – and went out leaving the door open. Barlow heard him open the front door and, with a shrug of the shoulders, got up himself and started doing up his coat. He pushed the envelope into his pocket, cast a regretful glance at the whisky bottle and walked out into the hall. Reynolds was in the act of closing the front door again. He looked up and saw Barlow's expression. Without a word he walked past him and back into the room. Barlow followed. Reynolds was standing beside his chair.

'Because I have respect for your reputation, I'll ignore that last remark. It sounded like nasty pressure.'

For a second Barlow's temper flared. Then he controlled it.

'I apologise,' he said stiffly. 'I agree it was. However, I had hoped you would be able to help me. I'm sorry. DC Edwards is outside. I mustn't keep him waiting.'

He turned towards the door but before he reached it he heard a clink of a glass. Reynolds' voice came over his shoulder.

'A pity. I was going to offer you a glass of Glenfiddich. And DC Edwards is not there. Rather than have him stationed outside my door for too long, I suggested he waited for you in the Masons' Arms.'

Still with his back turned, Barlow took a deep breath. His shoulders straightened and when he turned it was with all his old force and energy. He went back to his chair, sat down and took the glass that Reynolds was holding out to him.'

'Right, Mr Reynolds. Tell me.'

14

Fenton looked around the room. Everyone had arrived – except Barlow. He would have to start without him, which was irritating. The administrator in Fenton took control, and it was under his breath that he muttered his annoyance. Inquiries might be important but what was vital was to ensure that the overall machine ran smoothly. Despite the short notice and the fact that three of them had driven over two hundred miles, everyone had arrived promptly – everyone except Barlow who was somewhere out of reach in the suburbs of London.

Nevertheless, contriving to look as if Barlow's absence had been planned six months ago, Fenton coughed for attention, got it immediately, and addressed the meeting.

'Gentlemen. Thank you for making yourselves available at such short notice, particularly our colleagues from the Principality, who, I imagine, have been transgressing all manner of motorway speed limits in order to arrive on time.'

There were dutiful smiles around the table. The two men referred to grinned amiably and the Welshman who headed Number 8 District Regional Crime Squad acknowledged Fenton's remark with a mock salute. The Lancastrian, who was the head of Number 1 District which covered North Wales, said gaily, 'I'm admitting nothing.' Alongside him, one of Her

Majesty's Inspectors of Constabulary looked less amused. Fenton knew that he had had further to come and guessed that the drive might have had its hair-raising moments. He let his eyes move around the rest of the table. On his left, alongside the two Welsh representatives, sat a Deputy Assistant Commissioner from Scotland Yard and the National Co-ordinator of Regional Crime Squads. Across the table sat a senior representative of the Special Branch, and at the far end was a man Fenton had not met before, sent along by Military Intelligence. His rank was a matter for guesswork, since according to custom he had been introduced to the others simply as 'Mister'.

'You all know why we are here.' Fenton's gesture was so superfluous that no one even bothered to nod confirmation. 'Chief Superintendent Barlow who has been heading the investigation is still pursuing urgent inquiries. He will join us as soon as he can. Meanwhile I suggest we get on with it. First of all – could we have an outline of existing security precautions on this visit?'

He looked across towards the head of Number 8 District Regional Crime Squad, who cleared his throat. 'I'm speaking with the authority of Number One District too. Existing arrangements are not particularly elaborate. Nationalist objections to this particular reservoir have not been very strong. The valley in question was extremely thinly populated. It's historical and cultural associations were nil, and it isn't a place of any great beauty either. In fact, the general consensus was that it would look rather more attractive after it had been flooded than it did before.

'However,' he paused briefly and opened a file which lay on the table in front of him, 'since there is always the possibility of some hot-head throwing something, we went through the usual routine. Her Majesty will be coming from Shrewsbury where she has an engagement on the previous day. She will be travelling up the A5 for a distance of eighty miles. There are three danger spots on the route, apart from one section of three miles near the end of the route which is all vulnerable. Plainclothes men will be covering the first three points. Uniformed men will be stationed every two hundred yards along the last section. There will also be mounted officers patrolling the mountainside above, together with two dog teams. The whole area will be covered methodically two hours before the royal car is due. The site itself is fairly open. But there will be the usual police guard. There are three possible points from which a concealed sniper could operate. All three will be covered. What we cannot, at least on present strength, guard against is a sniper at long range out on the open hillside.'

Fenton looked around the table.

'Any questions.'

Before anyone could avail themselves of his offer, the Inspector of Constabulary held up his hand.

'If I may, Mr Fenton . . . Chief Superintendent Johnstone has given you the picture as it existed until we were given the information which has led to this meeting. What I now propose to do is to implement the detailed plan drawn up on the occasion of Her Majesty's attending Prince Charles' investiture at Caernarvon. You may remember, gentlemen, that there were grave doubts expressed at the time as to whether it was safe for Her Majesty to attend. It was the Chief Superintendent who was in charge on that occasion and it was acting on his assurance that the Palace decided to go ahead. In this case the requirement in terms of manpower will be marginally less since we shall not be required to cover a town like Caernarvon. But we shall nevertheless need to call upon the assistance of Lancashire Task Force, as we did then. I would also suggest that, as on that occasion, a further task force is held in readiness at the county border.'

Fenton glanced at the Deputy Assistant Commissioner, who nodded:

'I agree. We would also be prepared to make available a number of plainclothes officers and several dog teams as we did on that occasion.'

'Helicopters?'

The Regional Crime Squad chief answered.

'Yes. Already requested. Two from the air force and two from the army. A senior police officer as passenger in each one. In that sense we're lucky. We've got a blueprint ready at hand. All we have to do is adapt it slightly.'

'Yes,' Fenton sounded less sanguine. 'On the other hand, if our guesswork – and I concede it is only guesswork – is correct, we have a very real threat. Whereas previously we had only a vague possibility.'

He turned to the Special Branch man.

'What about the list of names your people have had?'

'It is being circulated at the moment to all regions with a request that a special watch be kept for the people on it. At the moment, all but four of the ones who live in London are still here. We've been keeping a very close eye on them for the past few days. Those four whom we would regard as leading figures in their various organisations all left London this morning.'

'Any idea where they were heading?'

The question came from the Welsh Crime Squad man.

'Your way,' was the laconic answer. 'Two of them caught trains to Cardiff. The other two left by car together. They booked into an hotel near Shrewsbury about three hours ago. Ten minutes ago they were drinking pints of bitter in the public bar.'

Fenton turned to Johnstone.

'What about your wild boys?'

Johnstone shrugged his shoulders.

'They're more or less where they ought to be. The trouble is that there are a dozen potential trouble-makers living within a few hours drive of that reservoir. None of them would need to start moving yet even if they were involved. But we're keeping tabs on the favourites.'

'Well', Fenton looked around the table. 'So much for the position as it stands. Action?'

Before anyone could answer there was a knock at the door.

'Ah!' Fenton got to his feet. 'This could be Barlow now.'

He went quickly across to the door and opened it. But instead of Barlow, a Home Office security man stood there. With him was an army despatch rider.

'I'm sorry to interrupt you, sir', he said. 'But the DR has an urgent message for Mr Wilson. To be delivered personally.'

The man from Military Intelligence got up and came across. Rapidly he took the envelope, signed the slip of paper the despatch rider held out to him and shut the door on the two men without ceremony. He tore open the envelope, skimmed through the contents and looked up at the others around the table.

'It's from our people in Belfast', he said. 'I put out a query and they thought this might be relevant. A gentleman connected with the Provisionals over there is reported to have left for Dublin. Apparently, the rumour is that he is coming to do a job over here. He's rather unusual in that he isn't Irish. In fact, he's a Frenchman – used to have OAS connections. After independence he went freelance.'

'Why should he be relevant to us, particularly?'

'Well, I gathered we thought a cracksman was involved. This man isn't a cracksman but he is something of a genius with explosives.'

There was a long silence. It was a mark of strain that Fenton's next remark was out loud and not under his breath.

'Where,' he said, looking around the table as if he might find the answer . . . 'Where the hell is Barlow?'

Barlow, in point of fact, was just finishing his second glass of Glenfiddich. Opposite him Reynolds was still sitting as calmly as if they had been discussing a possible change in the weather. Barlow put his glass down and glared angrily at the notes he had scribbled.

'Let me make sure I've got it right. The approach came through Meadows. You weren't told when but you were told that it was in North Wales . . . ? Right?'

'That's right,' Reynolds nodded. 'I was told that we would probably stay in Bangor and that it was only half an hour or so's drive from there.'

'Otherwise you weren't told anything about the job except the details that concerned you . . . Go through them again for me – I'll check against what I've got down here.'

Without any sign of impatience, Reynolds began to enumerate the facts he knew.

'It involved opening a large metal container which would be very heavy. No problem with stability. Its dimensions, from what I was told, were roughly eight feet by seven feet by seven feet. The sides and the lid were fourteen-inch-thick steel. The lid was fastened by bolts and a padlock. I had to get those off and then blow the lid. But the lid had to be blown by remote control. Meadows said it might have to be from a point two hundred yards away. He didn't say why and I didn't ask.'

'And he didn't tell you what was in it?'

'No. I didn't ask. They were offering a lot of money but I wasn't interested. As I told you, I don't particularly care for Mr Meadows and there was something slightly odd about this operation which didn't appeal to me. I am in a fortunate position. I can afford to choose my work.'

'And there's nothing else? Nothing at all?'

'Nothing else, Mr Barlow.'

'I'm very grateful to you, Mr Reynolds.' Barlow got up, pushed his notebook into his pocket. 'I'd like to stay but there are a number of very important gentlemen waiting for this information at this very moment. In fact, they've been waiting some time.' . . . He hesitated for a moment . . . 'I won't insult you by suggesting that it might be needed, Mr Reynolds. But if the occasion does ever arise and it might be of some help if word of this were to reach a judge . . .'

Reynolds acknowledged the offer with a dignified inclination of the head.

'That is very generous of you, Mr Barlow. I trust not. However, in this particular venture I'll wish you and your colleagues good hunting.'

Barlow was ushered out through the door and two minutes later a startled DC Edwards found himself forcibly extracted from the pub without being allowed to finish a good half-pint of beer left in his glass. Barlow didn't say a word on the journey back until they were nearly at the Home Office. Suddenly, he turned to Edwards.

'Are you any good at riddles?'

'Not bad, sir.'

'All right, then. Try this one. What is it that's within half an hour's drive of Bangor, measures eight feet by seven by seven, has sides of fourteen-inch-thick steel and is worth blowing the lid off?'

Edwards thought for a moment.

'I'm afraid I don't know, sir. That isn't the sort of riddle they have in Christmas crackers.'

'When I want a comedian I'll ask for one. I asked for a detective. You come from around that area, don't you?'

'Yes, sir.'

'Well, think, man. What is there within that range of Bangor?'

'Well, nothing really, sir. I mean – nothing that would interest someone like Danny Reynolds. There's the university. They do some secret rocket research. They might have some kind of chamber there that would fit.'

Barlow's only response was a grunt.

'I know it's not very likely, sir, but there's nothing really around Bangor. There are the quarries – they're within half an hour. There are explosive stores there. There's an electronics facory. Otherwise nothing at all. Then on Anglesey – most of that is within reach – there's the Rio Tinto plant, the RAF station at Valley. And that's it.'

As Edwards finished his catalogue, he drew up outside the Home Office. Barlow paused with his hand on the door.

'Nothing else?'

'No, sir.'

'Perhaps one of the high-powered gentlemen inside will be better at riddles. Report to me here – 9.30.'

Barlow marched up to the door and rang the night bell. Edwards put the car in gear and was about to drive off, then suddenly he wound down the passenger window and peered out.

'Mr Barlow?'

But the door was shutting. Barlow had gone. Edwards had remembered there was something else on Anglesey.

As Barlow pushed open the door, the six men around the table all swivelled towards him: he felt that the meeting had ground itself into a state of stagnation some time ago. A glance at Fenton confirmed his suspicion. In any other man, he would have interpreted the look on his face as that of someone who was pleased to see him. Fenton, being Fenton, contrived to banish his expression of relief almost as soon as it appeared.

'Good evening. Good of you to make it.'

'I'm sorry to be so late.' Barlow offered his apology briskly and moved to an empty place at the foot of the table.

'Your news, please. We are all agog.'

Barlow resisted the temptation to answer Fenton's irony with a magician's flourish. Instead he paused a moment, collected his thoughts and addressed the company generally.

'Gentlemen. My apologies for not attending this meeting from the outset. As Mr Fenton doubtless informed you, I have been pursuing inquiries which I hoped would provide some additional information. I have tracked down a person who was approached to take part in this enterprise but who turned the offer down. As a result of information which he provided me with we can narrow the inquiry very considerably.'

Barlow glanced across at a large map which hung on the wall behind Fenton's seat: 'The job whatever it is – lies within roughly half an hour's drive of Bangor in North Wales.'

They all automatically turned to stare at the map as if some magic formula would reveal the answer written there. It was the man from Military Intelligence, however, who pounced on the first half of Barlow's statement:

'You said "whatever it is"? You mean we still don't know?'

Barlow pushed back his chair, got up and walked over to the map.

'I'm hoping one of you gentlemen may be able to supply the answer. At the moment all I have is a riddle. According to my informant, the operation is in that area.' He traced a circle on the map. 'And the operation will involve – and I quote – opening a large and extremely heavy metal container, measuring some eight feet by seven, with sides and a lid of fourteen-inch-thick steel.'

There was a silence while the six other men returned Barlow's inquiring look with uniformly blank stares. Fenton coughed and it sounded like an explosion.

'Fourteen-inch-thick steel. That would imply that whatever those walls are protecting is extremely precious indeed.'

'One would think so.' Barlow shrugged. 'However, the detective constable who was with me and knows that area couldn't think of any building within the range that could contain a safe or a vault of that size.'

'And this is all this man could tell you?'

Despite his carefully neutral tone, Fenton's expression was that of a child who has seen a conjuror reach into his hat and fail to produce a rabbit.

'Nearly all.' Barlow glanced at his notes again. 'He did also say that he was told he would have to detonate whatever it is from a point two hundred yards away.'

The Military Intelligence officer got up and walked across to the map. He stared at it with obvious irritation.

'I haven't been in that area for some time. But to the best of my knowledge there is nothing there that could need that kind of protection. Whatever it is it would have to be immensely valuable . . .'

'Or dangerous' . . . The interruption came from the Welshman Johnstone. Abruptly he pushed his chair back and came to join the two men in front of the map. He stared at it intently for a moment or two and then said, half under his breath: 'It's got to be that. Got to be. There's nothing else.'

'What, man?'

It was Fenton who barked the question at him.

Slowly the other pointed his finger at a spot in a corner of Anglesey.

'That's the spot.'

'What's there, for God's sake?'

Barlow peered at the map. The only thing marked in appeared to be an ancient burial site.

The Welshman spoke very slowly and distinctly.

'That is the site of the Wylfa nuclear power station.'

The two standing alongside both stared at him. He didn't return their gaze but continued to look intently at the map. It was Barlow who reacted first.

'Yes,' he said softly. 'You're right. It has to be.'

Slowly the three of them turned away from the map and went back to their seats. Nobody said a word but by common consent all eyes turned to Fenton. The next move was his. Fenton glanced around at the faces. When he spoke his voice was flat and unemphatic.

'It would appear, therefore, that our friends are proposing to blow up a nuclear power station. Are we agreed that, on the basis of the information we have, that is the only conclusion to be drawn?'

Steadily his eyes moved from face to face around the table. At each pause he received a silent nod of confirmation. Once the circuit was complete, Fenton sat for a moment staring at the polished wood in front of him. His hand reached out for the phone. 'Switchboard? This is Fenton. I want to talk as soon as is humanly possible to the Chief Security Officer of the Atomic Energy Authority.'

Nobody said very much as they waited for the call to come through. The two Crime Squad Co-ordinators went into a huddle of their own. The Deputy Assistant Commissioner crossed to where Barlow was sitting, peering at his notes. They both looked at the scribbled figures together.

'I'm sure it is the power station', said Barlow eventually. 'But I don't think it's the central core, or whatever you call it. This thing has a lid with bolts on it. Reactor furnaces don't have lids.'

The other man nodded agreement.

'Some kind of storage place, perhaps? But it must contain nuclear material. What bothers me is what they're planning to do with it when they've got it.'

Barlow looked up at him sharply.

'You mean as opposed to just blowing it up?'

'That's right.'

'What else could they do with it?' said Barlow, although even as he asked he could think of the answer.

'The possibilities are endless. But the obvious one would be to blow it up somewhere else.'

The phone interrupted them before they could pursue the thought. Fenton reached for it quickly.

'Hello ... Yes. Sorry to disturb you at this hour. This is Fenton ... Yes I'm afraid it is urgent. So much so that I must ask you to come here ... to the Home Office ... Yes immediately ... We will explain that when you get here but I assure you that I am not making the request frivolously ... You have transport ... Excuse me a moment ...'

The Deputy Assistant Commissioner was holding up a hand to attract Fenton's attention.

'Ask him his address and one of our fellows will bring him here. It will be quicker.'

Fenton nodded agreement. After noting the address he was about to ring off when another thought struck him.

'Mr Ferguson? One other thing. We should like to talk to one of your scientists. A reasonably senior one ... Oh, someone who could tell us precisely what might happen if someone blew a part of a reactor up ... That's right ... Where would we find him? ... At Aldermaston itself ... And you know he's there now? Will you call him and ask him to stand by. Yes. A police-car will pick him up in ten minutes. Less if we can make it. Goodbye.'

The Assistant Deputy Commissioner was already talking into the other phone.

'Yes. That's right. A Mr Ferguson. To the Home Office. As fast as you like. And wait ...' He turned back to Fenton. 'And someone from Aldermaston?'

'Yes.' Fenton glanced at the sheet of paper in front of him. 'A Dr Henriques. He'll be waiting at the main gate. He's working late there this evening. Ferguson is contacting him for us.'

'Right.' The commissioner turned back to the phone. 'Marston? Get on to Thames Valley. Superintendent Richardson. My compliments. There is a Dr Henriques waiting at the main gate of Aldermaston Atomic Research Station. I want him picked up and brought to the Home Office. And Marston? ... Tell them to pull their fingers out.'

He had barely put the phone down before it rang again. It was Ferguson, the AEA security chief.

'Is Fenton there? ... Look, it doesn't matter. Can you tell him that Henriques has left his labs. I've spoken to his wife. She says that when he's working as late as this he usually stops for a drink in a pub just outside Maidenhead ... The Swan ...' The Yard man looked at his watch.

'It's gone ten thirty. That's closing time in that area.'

There was a chuckle at the other end of the line.

'Not at The Swan, apparently. Mrs Henriques says you go to the back door and knock.'

'Thank you very much. We'll do that.'

15

The knock on the door was a fairly loud one but, for a moment, nobody paid any attention. Instead they watched as a short, balding man in a green pullover stood with his final dart poised in his hand. He threw and landed it neatly in the double fifteen where it had been intended to go. There was a murmur of congratulation. The players moved to the bar and the landlord moved casually across to open the door. It was his muffled exclamation that made them all turn. The bar then became extremely silent as the two police officers pushed past him and into the bar.

The landlord hurriedly took up a position behind the bar.

'I know what you're thinking, gentlemen, but this is a private party. No money has changed hands. My wife is just preparing food in the kitchen. I assure you that that door has remained shut since . . .'

His words died away as the older of the two policemen waved him into silence:

'Count yourself lucky, mate. We're on other business.'

He looked around the bar.

'Is there a Dr Henriques here, please?'

One of the dart players stepped forward. He was tall with curly hair, heavy spectacles and a long, lean face. A full pint of beer was clutched in one hand and three darts in the other.

'Yes? I'm Henriques.'

'Would you come with us, sir? It's rather urgent but we'll explain in the car.'

'What's up? Trouble at the labs?'

'We'll explain in the car, sir.'

The policeman put an arm politely but firmly under Henriques' elbow and urged him towards the door. As they went out he turned back to the landlord.

'Sorry to break up the private party. But we're in a bit of a hurry. . . .' He paused with his hand on the door knob. 'But if I were you I wouldn't have another one tomorrow night. People might not understand.'

They vanished as rapidly as they had arrived, and a slightly shaken group were left staring at the door.

Henriques climbed into the patrol-car outside:

'Right. What's it about? How did you know I'd be there?' He chuckled. 'You gave Mr Hoskins the fright of his life anyway. He could see his licence vanishing in a puff of smoke.'

'Fortunately for him, sir, it's not our concern. We've been instructed to get you to London as fast as we can. So if you wouldn't mind sitting back in your seat, sir, we'll do just that.'

'To London? But what for . . . ?'

Henriques began to fire questions but he was flung back against the seat as, with a flurry of gravel, the patrol car leapt out of the yard and into the road, headlights blazing, blue light flashing and siren sounding. For the next couple of minutes he said nothing but watched in horrified fascination as the car hurtled around bends and across intersections. As it spun onto the motorway to London and settled into the fast lane scattering other motorists like sheep ahead of it, he found his voice again.

'Why London? Who wants me? Has my wife been told? She'll be expecting me shortly?'

The policeman who wasn't driving half turned his head.

'Your wife has been informed, I gather, sir. As for who wants you, we don't know. We had a message passed to us via the Yard that you were to be contacted and taken to the Home Office. I gather there's a bit of a flap on about something. So I'd just sit back and enjoy the ride, sir. I imagine they'll explain at the other end.'

It was reasonable advice and Henriques took it to the extent that he could, since the driver relentlessly held the car somewhere over the hundred mark and seemed perfectly prepared to risk ramming cars in front that were fractionally slow pulling over from the outer lane.

As a result it was a shaken and distinctly bewildered Dr Henriques who, a mere half hour after being about to start a game of darts at The Swan Inn, found himself facing a group of men in a room in the Home Office. It was some comfort when he turned his head and saw Ferguson, the security chief, sitting at the end of the table, though Ferguson had the air of a man out of his depth as well.

A dark-haired man with an icily handsome face came across to Henriques with his hand stretched out in introduction.

'Dr Henriques. Good evening. My name is Fenton and I am afraid that I am responsible for interrupting your drink. I assure you I wouldn't have done so unless it were important. I believe you know Mr Ferguson?'

Henriques nodded and Fenton continued around the table, ending with Barlow who had been watching the scientist's bemused face growing more and more baffled as police title followed police title to be followed by the cryptic phrase 'from the Ministry of Defence'. Barlow got up and moved over to Henriques.

'Dr Henriques, the reason you are here is quite simple. We have good reason to believe that a group of people are planning to blow up part of the nuclear power station at Wylfa. But we don't know which part. This is the information we have to go on.'

Once again, Barlow read out his riddle, paused and looked expectantly at Henriques. His brain had been sent reeling by

Barlow's opening words, but now he was within his own specialised field, it settled and began to function again.

'There is nothing inside Wylfa that corresponds to that description' he said.

'You're sure?' It was the man from the Ministry of Defence leaning forward, his eyes fixed on Henriques' face.

'Positive. I was one of the people who helped to design it.'

'Oh hell.' There was a crash as Barlow knocked a chair over in rage and disappointment. 'So we're back where we started from.'

Fenton got slowly to his feet, looking suddenly tired and grey.

'I'm sorry, Dr Henriques. We appear to have dragged you all this way on a wild goose chase.'

'No, wait a minute.' Henriques looked disconcerted. 'I only said there was nothing *inside* the power station that looks like that. I didn't say that it was nothing to do with the power station. That sounds to me like one of the containers used for shipping nuclear waste.'

There was no visible sign but suddenly all the nervous energy in the room which had been draining away started pumping up again. There was a scrape of a chair as the Regional Crime Squad chief pulled himself nearer to the table. Fenton's head lifted. His gaze was sharp and penetrating again. But it was Barlow who spoke first. He leant across and pulled out an empty chair next to him.

'Why don't you sit down and tell us?'

Henriques sat down, folded his hands in front of him and told them.

'Wylfa is a big nuclear power station. It isn't working at full capacity because there's a fault in it. We didn't allow for corrosion of some of the metal parts inside the thing. And they've also had trouble with the turbines. But, basically, it has two reactors, each of them with 49,000 thirty-pound fuel elements. During nuclear fission the Uranium 235 breaks down to form about 200 different "fission products". Most of these are highly radioactive. Each reactor core, I would say, has inside it about one hundred times the radioactivity that was released at Hiroshima.'

Henriques paused – to do him justice to collect his thoughts. Six pairs of eyes stayed fixed on his face.

'Now,' he said, 'When Wylfa is running steadily, in other words, when those damn turbines aren't giving trouble, the station will replace spent fuel elements at the rate of about 260 for each reactor every week. All those elements are full of fission products. Because radio-activity reduces with time, they stick them in a pond at the reactor site to cool off – just as you would a lump of molten steel, say, if you didn't want to carry it about while it was hot. When they're about red hot, they're put – about 200 elements at a time, weighing two and a half tons – in a socking great steel box filled with water, which weighs about fifty tons. I think the exact weight is forty-eight tons. The details you read out to me are a pretty accurate description of one of those boxes.'

Fenton cut in sharply.

'What happens to these "boxes", as you call them?'

Henriques looked surprised that anyone should ask so obvious a question.

'They go to British Nuclear Fuels at Windscale. They sort them out there, extract the uranium and plutonium that we can use again and dump the rest.'

This time it was Barlow who prodded him.

'How do they go?'

Henriques nodded towards Ferguson, the security officer.

'I think you'd better ask him. He is probably more up to date than I am on the details of the movement.'

As all the eyes swung towards him, Ferguson looked deeply unhappy but, without waiting for any further prompting, started to speak.

'We send two or three of these boxes or casks as we call them from Wylfa by road on a low-load lorry. They go along the A5025 to a railhead at Valley. They travel at a maximum speed of ten miles an hour. From Valley they travel by rail to Windscale.'

'What are the security arrangements for that road journey?'

The question came from Barlow. Ferguson contrived to look even unhappier.

'Well, there aren't any really.'

'What!'

There was an incredulous chorus around the table. Ferguson looked around him and obviously decided that a man who can go down no further might as well try and fight his way back up.

'Look, gentlemen, it's all very well for you to sit here with hindsight and sound deeply shocked. But the fact remains that we have never seen any need for special security arrangements. Obviously those low-loaders have the normal police escort for large dangerous loads. But we have never seen any need to surround them with men with machine-guns. After all, why should anyone want to hijack them? What could they do with them anyway?'

Fenton felt that the moment had arrived for an exercise in chairmanship.

'Mr Ferguson has raised a valid question.' He turned to Henriques. 'Dr Henriques, as our own hijacked expert, can you tell us in layman's terms what someone could do with that load, assuming they managed to get hold of it?'

Henriques thought for a moment.

'They'd have to blow it up. The only trouble is that the really nasty stuff – the radio-active Iodine 135 which would come out of the can as a vapour – will have lost a lot of its nastiness in the cooling-off period. They'll have to rely on solids like Strontium 90 and Cesium 137.'

He stopped for a moment and stared thoughtfully at the ceiling. The others watched while he concentrated on his macabre hypothesis.

'If I were them,' said Henriques, and Barlow had to hide a grin at the serious, academic tone 'I would take the bolts and padlocks off the lid, pack explosive around it and then detonate the explosive from a nice, safe distance. I should think about two hundred yards would be safe enough' ... He paused for a moment and then swung his head to look at Barlow.

'Would I have access to a mortar?'

'A mortar?' Barlow blinked and then recovered rapidly. 'Yes, I should think so, if you wanted one.'

'In that case,' said Henriques, beaming as happily as if the scheme really were his, 'I would fire a few mortar bombs into the thing just to get a really good fire going. Then I would leave rather hurriedly.'

It was Fenton who cut across the somewhat schoolboy atmosphere that Henriques had unwittingly created.

'What would happen then, Dr Henriques?'

Henriques' temporary euphoria fell away from him.

'If there were a reasonable wind, I would say that there would be a swathe of countryside that would be totally uninhabitable for about a hundred miles. Even if there were no wind, that would mean that all the fall-out would descend on Holyhead and the surrounding districts. I believe the population of Holyhead is somewhere in the region of 12,000.'

'And they would all be dead?'

'They wouldn't all die at once. But I would hate to see the cancer and leukaemia figures in twenty or thirty years time.'

A match scraped along a matchbox, and everyone else in the room tensed and then rather sheepishly relaxed. No one spoke for a full minute. Then, diffidently, the man from Military Intelligence turned to Henriques.

'You've been talking solely in terms of a local explosion. But what if they decided to take this low-loader somewhere after they had hijacked it? Could they contrive a situation where it was highly dangerous for anyone, however well organised, to take it away from them?'

'Not really, no. You see, they wouldn't really be able to present themselves as a total menace just by blowing the lid off the cask. The nasty stuff would still be shut away in its metal cans. They would have to explode those as well to release the radioactive material. And anyone who stayed close to that cask after the lid was off would be dead from acute radiation sickness within hours' ... Henriques stared thoughtfully at Fenton who returned his gaze. 'I suppose it would depend whether you had straightforward criminals or fanatics ...' He paused again, allowing his unspoken question to hang in the air. It was Fenton who answered him.

'That is the problem, Dr Henriques. We may well have both.'

'Oh.' For the first time since he had entered the room, Henriques looked genuinely frightened. 'In that case,' he stopped abruptly and gnawed at a thumb-nail ... 'In that case ... If they had two men, say, prepared to sit on that lid, ready to blow it off and explode the contents. Then I would be scared stiff to go anywhere near them. Even if they took it all the way down the A6 to Piccadilly Circus.'

16

At seven in the morning Barlow was spluttering and whale-blowing under a cold shower in the Home Office. A duty driver had gone to his flat and returned with fresh linen and a different suit, and Barlow was even cheerful as he stepped briskly into Dean Ryle Street and round the corner to the best workmen's cafe in Westminster.

He ate hungrily as he pondered again the plan he and the Welsh Regional Crime Squad chief had concocted during the night. It was foolproof, and it was calculated to make Fenton wreck every piece of paper on his desk.

Promptly at nine he arrived in Fenton's office. The others, however, were already there, all of them looking slightly grey and worn. Fenton opened proceedings in his usual brisk fashion.

'Right, gentlemen. I should tell you that I spoke to the Minister earlier this morning and effectively ruined his breakfast. He stressed that whatever approach we adopt to solve this problem – and he was gratifyingly content to leave the details to this meeting – there must be no risk to civilian life whatsoever. He was insistent on that point. I must say I agree with him. Apart from anything else, the psychological set-back to Britain's nuclear energy programme would be enormous.'

Fenton paused and coughed rather hurriedly, feeling perhaps that he had betrayed an over-impersonal concern with larger issues. He turned to the man from Military Intelligence.

'Your people have tabs on a good many of the men we feel are involved in this. How soon could you guarantee to have them all rounded up?'

'I would say, given *carte blanche*, within twenty-four hours.' He produced a file from his case. 'I checked with our people in the early hours of this morning. Naturally, general surveillance was stepped up as soon as things looked as though they were coming to a head. We can't guarantee that we can pick up every single one involved. But by casting the net fairly wide we can cripple any plans they have in mind.'

'Good.' Fenton straightened a pencil briskly and turned to the Deputy Assistant Commissioner.

'The problem, obviously, is then how long we – or rather you – can hold them. My opinion is that we should risk a possibly damaging action for false arrest rather than run the greater risk of allowing anyone we even remotely suspect to be at liberty.'

The Yard man looked vaguely unhappy, but the answer was diplomatic:

'We have had one or two unfortunate experiences in this area. The Angry Brigade trial, for example. And there would be more people involved this time. I would be a great deal happier if we could piece together a general charge of conspiracy rather than going at it piecemeal.'

Fenton nodded agreement.

'The details I would leave to you and your colleagues – and subject to the guidance you would seek from the Director of Public Prosecutions.' He glanced across at the Welsh detective. 'You will have to deal independently, of course. But I imagine that the people we're talking about will have stepped out of line on other occasions, sufficiently to give you reasonable grounds?'

The Superintendent nodded.

'Oh yes. There are enough defacing signpost charges to stretch from here to Bangor. We don't usually like making too many martyrs. But given these special circumstances we could bring in pretty well everyone on the list.'

Fenton turned back to Military Intelligence.

'What about our Irish cracksman friend? How do we take care of him?'

'I think the best thing is for one of my men to go and have a chat to him. We have been keeping tabs on him. He's staying in an hotel just outside Aberystwyth at the moment. There's nothing we can charge him with. But, on the other hand, he's a careful man and he's also a man who feels allegiance to Ireland. He's over here just on a kind of a lend-lease arrangement. If he knows that we're onto his new colleagues – and that there's a risk he may get picked up and be lost to the Irish – then I think he'll pull out without any compunction.'

Fenton looked around the table with an expression of satisfaction.

'Well, I must say that seems neat enough. Is there anything we have overlooked?'

There was a silence. Then Barlow lifted a hand.

'Mr Barlow?' Fenton raised an eyebrow in his direction. 'You want to say something?'

'Yes, I do.' Barlow rested his forearms on the table and looked slowly around the group. 'I think, if you'll forgive me, we are going about this in entirely the wrong way.'

In the stillness that followed the remark, Fenton's eyes hardened. 'Explain yourself.'

'I intend to.' Barlow returned the look. 'I am a policeman. I'm talking like a policeman now. My job is to catch criminals and to catch them properly in the circumstances which ensure that they will be properly convicted of their crime. I don't think I would be doing my job by rounding up a number of people who I know were intending to commit a serious crime, locking them up for a couple of days and then letting them all go again. We might stop them this time. But what about next time? Our job is to stop this little lot once and for all. And that's what I want to do.'

Nobody spoke for a moment and then Johnstone, addressed himself to Fenton.

'May I say, sir, that I agree with Mr Barlow. These men are villains – and our job is to catch villains – not just put obstacles in their path.'

Fenton looked unconvinced and irritated.

'Do I take it then, Charles, that you are suggesting. . . .' He let his words trail away but nodded understanding.

'Yes. I am suggesting that we let them go ahead with their plan and catch them at it. That way we stop them once and for all.'

The man from Military Intelligence cut in.

'What Barlow is advocating involves a considerable element of risk and a totally unnecessary one. We can pick these fellows up, let them know we're onto them and they would never dare try it again.'

'But you can't be sure of that. You certainly can't be sure they won't go and try something else. And we may not have advance warning next time. This is police-work, and that means catching them, not trying to get them fourteen days for putting green paint on road signs or being in possession of cannabis.

'Besides, you talk about risk. What risk? We know what the job is, we know when it's going to happen – or we shall know when that low-loader is leaving. We know the villains involved. We just sit back and wait for them to walk into it.'

'And if something goes wrong?' Fenton shot the question at Barlow. 'If something goes wrong, Barlow? You heard Dr Henriques? A hundred miles of countryside uninhabitable. What if they let it off near Birmingham or London? I cannot take that risk.'

Fenton got to his feet to indicate that he regarded the matter as closed. Barlow stayed in his seat.

'I'm sorry. But you put me in charge of this investigation and I intend to see it carried out properly. You spoke of taking chances.

May I point out that if we adopt your suggestion we shall be taking a much bigger chance – the chance that next time they may succeed – and we are also guaranteeing that there will be a next time. I am suggesting that we finish this thing once and for all.'

Slowly and reluctantly Fenton sat down again. He looked across at the Deputy Assistant Commisioner.

'Would you care to give us your opinion?'

The DAC got up and walked across to the wall map. He stood in front of it for a moment, looking at the point where the nuclear power station at Wylfa had been circled in red, then turned to face the others.

'I agree with you, sir, that there is a risk. There always is in this kind of operation.' He held a hand up to forestall a protest from Barlow, who had allowed an angry growl to escape. 'No, Barlow, there is. Things can go wrong. They have gone wrong in the past and they will go wrong again. What is more, the penalties of failure in this instance would be enormous. I firmly believe that there is a fanatical element involved and that what they have in mind for that container is something far more spectacular than an explosion in the middle of Anglesey. What is more, if they do get in a position to carry out their threat, there appears to be no way of dislodging them.'

He turned away from the map and walked back to his seat.

'In that case,' Fenton started collecting his papers together, 'we appear to have a clear consensus . . .'

The DAC coughed politely but firmly.

'I am sorry, Mr Fenton, but I had not finished. I merely said that I was fully aware of the risks involved. However, I also feel we should remember that if we adopt preventative measures, we shall have scotched the snake, not killed it. We shall be facing a continual and unknown threat of something similar or possibly even more extreme occurring at some future date.'

He turned to Fenton suddenly as if his mind was finally made up.

'I agree with Barlow. I think we have to treat this as we would any criminal operation. We have to take enormous care to ensure success. But we have to act as we would normally. We must catch these men in the act of committing the crime we know they intend to commit.'

Fenton said nothing. He stared at the table in front of him. Then he looked up at Barlow.

'Earlier this morning I gave an assurance to the Minister that there would be absolutely no risk to civilian life. Can you give me that same assurance?'

'Yes.' Barlow's stare was as challenging as Fenton's own. 'The criminals will be at risk. So will the police. But there will be no risk to the public at large.' For a full thirty seconds Fenton held the look and then, abruptly, stood up.

'In that case, Mr Barlow, you are in charge. Keep me informed.'

He swept his papers together and left the room. As the door closed behind him Barlow let out a long, slow breath. Then he turned to the others.

'Gentlemen, I suggest that those of us directly concerned adjourn to my office. We have work to do.'

'Do you need me, Barlow?' It was the Assistant Commissioner who asked the question.

'No, sir. However, I would be grateful for two things.'

'Name them.'

'I'd like that young DC Edwards I had last night.'

'Certainly. Second thing?'

'I want the services of the six best marksmen that Scotland Yard can provide.'

'I see.' The DAC did not look particularly surprised. 'It's going to be like that, is it?'

'Yes, sir. It's going to be like that.'

17

'All right. Pay attention.'

Barlow stood facing the forty men crowded into the parade room in Bangor police station. As he looked at them he thought that, at least, they represented an interesting exercise in police co-operation. Apart from the half dozen men from the Yard, sitting in front of him were hand-picked men from no fewer than four Task Forces. Outside in the car park were sitting six of the best and most experienced police-dogs, all of them with a record of successfully bringing down armed men. If he couldn't pull it off with this lot, thought Barlow. . . . Then he pushed the thought aside. There were no 'ifs' possible this time.

'I'm going to say all this once. I don't want to have to say it again. But if anyone isn't clear about anything when I've finished, then for God's sake say so. On this job, we can't afford to take any chances at all.'

He turned to a map drawn on the board behind him.

'Right. This is the route the low-loader will take. Edwards and Griffiths will be driving it. They will be locked in. From our survey we reckon there are two possible points where the hi-jacking could take place. We have decided to eliminate one of them. A dozen of you, you know who you are already, will be dressed as council workmen attempting to dig the road up at one of the spots. You will also serve as a reserve force should we need you. So stay in continuous radio contact. We shall all be using ultra-high-frequency apparatus – that should prevent casual radio eavesdropping. And you road-workers, have your vehicles at the ready. You will have two Liverpool Task Force undercover cars which will look ordinary enough, so you can park them right alongside you.

'The low-loader will be followed by two other unmarked cars and a local delivery van which we have borrowed for the occasion. That will contain the dogs. Now obviously these vehicles cannot get too close. On the other hand, I am assuming that these fellows reckon that it's only going to take them a couple of minutes to do the job, so they won't bother to check vehicles more than a mile or so behind the low-loader. We shall follow it at a distance of two miles. It will be up to Edwards and Griffiths to hold them off until we get there. It shouldn't be too difficult. A locked cab isn't all that easy to get into, particularly when you are expecting it to be open.

'However, help – with luck – will be even nearer at hand. We are assuming – and I think it's a reasonable assumption, that the hijack will take place here.' Barlow stabbed a finger at the map. 'It is the only spot which has woodland alongside and gives some kind of cover. Everywhere else is wide open. Quarter of a mile ahead of it is a farm. Two vehicles with a full complement of officers will be parked out of sight there. They should be on the spot within twenty seconds or so. They will also have dogs with them.

'The first warning, hopefully, even before we hear from Edwards and Griffiths, will come from the helicopter. This will obviously not be overhead. In fact, it will be cruising about a mile away. But Inspector Jackson will be on board, equipped with a pretty powerful pair of field-glasses. He should be able to spot any activity the moment they start to leave cover.'

One of the Scotland Yard officers put his hand up.

'Yes?'

'Won't the helicopter make them suspicious, just tacking up and down like that?'

'No.' Barlow made no attempt to hide his impatience. 'For one thing it won't be tacking up and down. It will be flying steadily at an angle to the road as if it were on a routine flight. Furthermore, there is an aerodrome with Air Sea Rescue helicopters a couple of miles away. People round there are more surprised if they don't see helicopters about. And our villains have local assistance. They won't worry about a helicopter. Any more questions? No. Right. The low-loader is scheduled to leave at 14.00 hours. I want everybody in position within one hour from now. I shall be in the first car following. All radio contact will be through me. Call signs are in the written instructions you will be given as you leave. That's all, gentlemen. And remember. On this operation there can be no mistakes – no mistakes at all.'

There was a scrape of feet and a murmur of voices as the men left. Barlow turned to Johnstone who was standing alongside him. Johnstone gave him a reassuring pat.

'Come on, Charles. What we both need is one quick, stiff drink and then off we go.' Barlow nodded. He said nothing, however, as Johnstone led him into a next-door office and produced a bottle of whisky from a cupboard.

'Emergency supplies,' he said, pouring them both a generous measure. 'I don't know about you but I'm nervous.'

Barlow took his drink and sipped it slowly.

'Yes.'

He looked up at Johnstone.

'You did check? Edwards and Griffiths are both single men?'

'Yes, I did.'

'Well, that's something.'

Abruptly Barlow picked up his drink and poured the rest of it down his throat.

'Come on, let's go.'

They walked to the car in silence. But as they stood with their hands on the doors, Barlow looked hard at Johnstone.

'Wait a minute.'

He turned and lumbered at a fast trot across the yard to where the main group was assembled. Johnstone saw him speaking urgently to two of the senior officers and then he was on his way back. He climbed into the car looking slightly more cheerful. Johnstone looked enquiringly at him.

'Last-minute inspiration?'

'No,' said Barlow. But I've made a change. I've pulled Griffiths out of the cab and arranged to put one of the dogs inside, with his handler. A lad called Andrews. He's single too.'

Johnstone looked at him.

'You're not absolutely certain this thing is going to work, are you?'

There was a long silence.

'No', said Barlow. 'I'm not certain at all. Do you know what I reckon is in it?'

'Tell me.'

'About fifteen seconds – either way.'

18

Never before had Barlow realised that ten miles an hour was so slow. The two cars and the van were pulled into a side-road a mile from the power station, as they watched the low-loader crawl past them. Then the radio crackled at him.

'Blue One to Red One.'

It was the helicopter.

'Red One.'

'Quarry in sight, sir. Just where we expected them. Two men hidden from the road. One of them has field-glasses. Just above the ambush spot.'

'Red One to Blue One. Well done. See if you can spot the rest.'

Barlow put the receiver down and the cars slid out of the side-road to start their slow procession. The low-loader was out of sight but they could hear its engine grinding away somewhere ahead of them.

For what seemed like hours they crawled along. Barlow leant forward and picked up the handset.

'Red One to Blue One.'

'Blue One. Yes, sir?'

'Any sign of the rest of them?'

'No, sir.' Jackson sounded slightly worried. 'We've circled

round and done another sweep. The two of them are still there but I can't see any sign of anyone else.'

'All right. Keep looking.'

Barlow turned to find Johnstone was already staring worriedly at him.

'He should have spotted them by now.'

'I'd have thought so.'

Barlow gazed out of the window with an appearance of calm. It was Johnstone who put the unspoken thought into words.

'That is, of course, assuming they are there.'

Barlow said nothing but he pressed doggedly on.

'Those two could be just look-outs.'

By way of answer, Barlow picked up the handset again.

'Red One to Blue Two.'

'Blue Two.' It was Edwards' voice, shouting to make himself heard over the roar of the low-loader's engine.

'State your position, Blue Two.'

'Blue Two to Red One. Approximately one mile from the ambush point.'

Barlow put his hand over the receiver and spoke to their driver.

'How far are we behind them?'

'Exactly two miles, sir. We've been maintaining constant speed.'

'Red One to Blue Two. Anything unusual?'

'Blue Two to Red One. Nothing at all. Only the dog.'

'Red One to Blue Two.' Barlow snapped it out. 'What's wrong with the dog?'

There was a chuckle from the receiver.

'Car-sick, sir.'

'Red One to Blue Two. Stop making jokes and watch the hedges. Out.'

Barlow threw the receiver onto the seat beside him and stared ahead as if willing something to happen. Johnstone tried to lighten the atmosphere a little.

'Well, at least they're feeling cheerful.'

All he got in reply was a grunt as the convoy of cars crawled forward another hundred yards, their engines barely turning over in first gear. Suddenly the receiver crackled.

'Blue One to Red One.'

Barlow grabbed at the receiver.

'Yes, Blue One?'

Inspector Jackson's voice sounded half puzzled, half apologetic:

'Blue One to Red One . . . I'm sorry if it's none of my business, sir. But when did you divide the road-gang?'

'Red One to Blue One. Explain.'

'Well, they are divided, sir. I can see the main group exactly in position. But then there's another lot of them about three-quarters of a mile further down the road.'

'Red One to Blue One. Where is the second road-gang? Exactly.'

'Blue One to Red One. I should say almost precisely three-quarters of a mile further down the road. The low-loader is about a hundred yards short of them now.'

Barlow felt the sweat prickling on his forehead. He hunched forward over the hand-set and spoke rapidly and distinctly into it.

'Red One to all Blue cars. Red One to all Blue cars. The action is a mile further east. Repeat. The action is a mile further east. Proceed at speed. Repeat. Proceed at speed.' He clapped his hand over the set for a second and shouted to his own driver.

'Pull over. Let the others through.'

Then he swung back to the hand-set.

'Red One to Blue Two. Red One to Blue Two. The road-gang ahead of you. Repeat. The road-gang ahead of you. Acknowledge . . .' He paused but the set was silent. 'I repeat. Acknowledge'. Suddenly the set came to life. But all they could hear over it was the snarling sound of a dog – and the crash of breaking glass.

Edwards and the dog handler, Andrews, had had no warning at all. It had barely dawned on Edwards that this particular road-gang was in the wrong place when its members had swung round from the trench they were leaning over and come racing towards the low-loader. A pick-handle which suddenly had no pick on the end crashed into Edwards' window before he even had time to draw his gun, and he went down from a second blow that took him across the head. The dog-handler was more fortunate. The first man to vault onto his side aimed his blow too hurriedly and caught the side of the door-frame. The second blow came almost at once but by then Andrews' gun was out. He fired at point-blank range into the head and shoulders that came heaving into the cab. There was a gasp and the head lurched back out of sight and fell away. A shot fired from the roadside hit the back of Andrews' seat. There was a sound of wrenching metal, and he felt his door buckling as someone tore at it from the outside. Behind him he was dimly aware of Edwards' body slumped against him. But the dog was holding his own. There was a snarl and then a scream. The dog lurched back against Andrews, then threw itself forward again. He just had time to notice there was blood staining its jaw when a body launched itself through the window and two arms locked themselves around his head and neck. There was no time to aim. He just pushed his gun upwards against a body and fired. It became a dead weight, and as he struggled to push it back out through the window, he heard tearing metal and felt the cab door begin to go.

In the third vehicle Barlow was crouched forward beating his fist pointlessly against the dashboard as the car flung itself around the corner. Ahead of them stood the low-loader. Around and on top of it was raging a small war. Barlow's eyes swept over the scene. Six men, two of them from the normal police motor-cycle escort, were lying in the road. Another shot rang out and a man on top of the low-loader slid to the ground. Beside the driver's door three men were forcing their way in. On the other side a body, Barlow couldn't see whether it was Andrews or not, was being dragged backwards through the window by two men, while two more were wrenching at the door itself with crowbars. At either side of the lorry a group of men was mixed up in a flurry of fighting bodies. Two dogs were lying whimpering. Alongside Barlow, Johnstone, his voice hoarse with panic, said in a strangled whisper:

'Christ, they're going to do it!'

As they watched, the two cars ahead of them shrieked to a halt a few yards short of the end of the low-loader. From the van the dog-handlers tumbled out, the dogs running silently and low, but they and the men keeping well into the side of the hedge. From the cars, however, the men did not come running. Instead all four of them jumped out and stood rock-steady. From behind they looked as if they were standing calmly at ease just watching the scene before them. But almost at once there was a sharp, flat crack of weapons. One of the two men wrenching at the cab's left-hand door staggered back clutching his shoulder. The other pitched forward and lay still. There was another concentrated report as all four guns fired virtually together, and the group which had been trying to pull the man free suddenly broke and ran, one of them dragging a leg.

There was a word of command, and the dogs went silently past the low-loader and after them. But even as they ran past, there was another report, this time a single one, and the dog which had been framed in the window fell back into the cab. With a heave one of the attackers wrenched himself upwards and hung poised half in and half out. Johnstone saw the nearest marksman swing round. Minutes seemed to go by while he steadied himself and took aim. Two other men on the road below jumped at the cab. But as they did so there was a shot. The body they had been trying to heave into the cab slid slowly backwards on top of them and carried them to the ground. As suddenly as it had begun, it was all over.

Barlow walked forward, put a hand on a policeman's shoulder and lifted himself up to look into the cab. Edwards was lying spread-eagled across the back of the seat. A hideous wound in the back of his head was slowly pulsing blood. For a second Barlow couldn't see Andrews, then he found him. He had a gash across his forehead with blood running down the side of his face. One arm was hanging limp by his side, the other was cradling the dog which lay with its head in his lap. The dog was breathing hoarsely with a hole torn in its chest. As Barlow's shadow fell across him, Andrews looked up at him.

'He did all right, didn't he, sir? Considering he was car-sick.'

Barlow said nothing for a moment, just looked at them both. Then he nodded gravely.

'For a dog that was car-sick he did very well indeed.'

19

As Barlow got back to his own car, Johnstone was waiting for him.

'It isn't as bad as it looked,' he said. 'The ambulances are on the way but all our people should pull through.'

Barlow nodded towards the low-loader.

'There are three of them in there that need help. Two from a doctor, the other from a vet. Take over, will you?' he added, opening the car door.

Johnstone looked at him in astonishment.

'Why? Aren't you coming back to the station? There are all these fellows to be charged, and the reports . . .' His voice tailed away as he watched Barlow climb into the car. Barlow wound the window down and leant across.

'You take care of it. I'm off. I'll be in touch.'

He raised a hand and before Johnstone could even begin to ask any more questions, the car was accelerating down the road. Johnstone watched it turn the corner and, with a shrug of the shoulders, turned away.

In the car, Barlow reached for the radio. Once he had been put through to the local Task Force, he rattled off a string of instructions, then turned to the driver.

'Wake me up when we're ten miles north of Oxford.'

The driver turned his head to ask a question but Barlow showed every sign of being fast asleep.

He woke in time to give the driver explicit directions. They left the main road and headed towards Woodstock. After a while they turned off again down a side-road that wandered between hedges for a couple of miles. Eventually they approached stone pillars with a pair of handsome stone lions perched on them. Barlow didn't need to tell the driver that this was their destination: two police cars were parked across the drive-way, effectively preventing any vehicle entering or leaving. As Barlow drew up alongside, a uniformed inspector came across to them.

'Mr Barlow?'

Barlow nodded towards the drive.

'Anybody tried to leave?'

'No, sir. Only one local delivery van called as well. We followed instructions, so he didn't get in.'

'Good. Pull over, will you? I'm going up to the house. Follow me, and park round the side.'

The drive was somewhat less imposing than the approach suggested, but the house was pleasant enough: the residence of a country gentleman with income enough to maintain it and its surrounding lawns. A well-disciplined creeper displayed itself across half the frontage, and through the wide Georgian windows there was a glimpse of a light, airy interior. With a crunch of gravel Barlow's car stopped carefully in front of the main door. Barlow got out and rang the bell. He heard brisk footsteps approaching and the door was opened. Standing there was a man in his middle forties, casually dressed in sports coat and cavalry twill trousers. His face was pleasant, slightly weather-beaten, his hair greying but carefully cut. He looked as if he went with the house. The two men stood in silence for a moment, inspecting each other. Barlow spoke first.

'Mr Meadows, I presume?'

'Yes, I'm Meadows.' The voice was flat, unemphatic but controlled. 'Are you the man who put the watchdogs on my gate?'

'Just a precaution, Mr Meadows. I wanted to have a chat with you, and since you've not long been back and since I've driven quite a long distance, I wanted to make sure of finding you at home.'

'Well now, you have, haven't you?'

Meadows' tone remained perfectly courteous but he made no move to invite Barlow into the house. Barlow solved the problem by walking past him and into the hall. Once inside he paused and looked around.

'This is very pleasant. You've obviously taken a great deal of trouble with it. Where shall we talk?'

He opened a door and peered into the room.

'How about in here? I see it's where you were sitting when I arrived.'

Without waiting for an answer he marched in and sat down. Meadows, looking amused rather than annoyed, followed him.

'Do make yourself at home, Mr . . . er . . . ?'

'Detective Chief Superintendent Barlow.'

'Ah yes . . . You're not attached to the local force.' He might have been a lord lieutenant making conversation before handing out a life-saving medal.

'No,' said Barlow. 'As I said, I've driven quite a long way. In fact, from Anglesey. There was an attempt to hijack a low-loader carrying nuclear waste there this morning.'

'Good heavens.' Meadows contrived to look mildly alarmed. 'How very unpleasant! Were the . . . er . . . thieves successful?'

There was a pause before Barlow answered.

'No.'

Meadows relaxed slightly in his chair but kept his eyes fixed on Barlow's face. 'But this, as you yourself pointed out, is some way from Anglesey. What brought you to me?'

'Because you organised it, Meadows.' Barlow held up a hand to forestall an interruption, although Meadows showed no sign of making one. 'Still, saying that and proving it are two very different things, as you well know. But I couldn't resist the pleasure of coming here personally to tell you that your nasty little idea for making money by terrifying half the country out of its wits didn't work.'

Meadows jumped to his feet and took a couple of steps towards Barlow's chair. Barlow too jumped to his feet and stood waiting for him.

Meadows stood very still, staring at Barlow, and then slowly, visibly, he relaxed and walked back to his chair. Settling himself into it, he said in a carefully conversational tone:

'I assume that you have some better reason for coming to see me?'

'Yes, I do.' Barlow too went back to his chair. 'Your lads made a mess of it, Meadows.'

'But why come and see me? Curiosity? Yes, I think that's probably it.' Meadows reached out an arm and took a cigarette from a box beside his chair. He looked across at Barlow, a smile curling his lips.

Barlow smiled in reply. 'You're right. How about satisfying that curiosity?'

'You have to be joking. I should help – '

Barlow smiled again. 'There are no witnesses. You can deny this conversation ever took place.'

Meadows sneered: 'You're not wired for sound?'

'I'm old fashioned. And how would a recording help me? I've not cautioned you. I don't mean to caution you because I know I've no evidence with which to charge you. So – satisfy my curiosity.'

'You want to know what I was doing involved with such odd company, don't you?'

Barlow looked suddenly stony faced.

'The question had crossed my mind.'

'Well, I think it was something of an inspiration on my part.' Meadows stretched out his legs and looked thoughtfully at his feet. 'Just between these four walls, I don't mind telling you that. You see, it occurred to me as I kept on reading in the newspapers about these young hot-heads that what they really lacked was organisation, a little financial backing, and pointing in the right direction. Given that, they could be transformed into quite a useful weapon – in the right hands. Because they do have one enormous advantage over professional criminals. They are extremely enthusiastic and they work for practically nothing.'

'They also don't always pull it off.'

'So I gather.' Meadows blew smoke reflectively at the ceiling. 'Still, the scheme was a good one. If they had managed to hi-jack that infernal load, they could have driven it to the outskirts of Birmingham. The thought was to charge a ransom of a million pounds. In return for my, shall we say, contribution, which involved an investment of £2,000, they agreed to allow me one third of the profits. You can only make that kind of bargain with idealists.'

'What were the arrangements for handing over the ransom?' Barlow asked the question with the interested air of someone listening to his host discuss his particular hobby.

'I don't think I'll tell you that. After all, as you say, you may have locked up some of my new recruits this morning. But there are plenty more where they came from and, who knows, I might want to use the technique again some time. And now if you'll excuse me . . .'

He began to move towards the door. Barlow got up from his seat and followed him out into the hall. Meadows opened the front door and stood to one side. Barlow walked slowly forward and paused on the threshold. Meadows started to close the door but stopped when he realised Barlow was still blocking the way. A note of impatience crept into his voice.

'Good afternoon, Mr Barlow.'

Barlow appeared not to hear. Instead he put both fingers in his mouth and let out a piercing whistle. From around the corner of the house the two patrol-cars came into sight. They rolled to a stop just in front of the door. Six policemen, led by the inspector, got out and stood looking inquiringly up at Barlow. He stood aside and motioned with his head. In a well-drilled group they marched into the house and stood expectantly in the hall. Barlow spoke to the inspector.

'Turn this place over.'

A gleam of appreciation shone in the inspector's eye.

'Yes, sir.'

Meadows grabbed Barlow's arm.

'Now wait a minute . . .'

His protest was cut short in a gasp of pain as Barlow's hand slammed down onto his wrist. Before he could recover, Barlow had taken him by both lapels of his jacket and was shaking him very slowly from side to side.

'Don't you touch me, Meadows. I'm warning you – don't give me any excuse at all. I've seen half a dozen good men carried off in ambulances today – and you put them there.'

He turned his head to look at the inspector.

'Don't stand there. Get on with it.'

The inspector saluted smartly: 'Which warrant, sir?'

Barlow was heading back into the room, propelling Meadows in front of him. He didn't even bother to look round: 'Any one.'

Meadows swung round, and the inspector was prepared. 'We have the warrants, sir. Mine permits me to search for dangerous drugs under Section 14, Subsection 2, of the Dangerous Drugs Act, the Sergeant's for offensive weapons under Section 26 of the Firearms Act, 1968, and PC Pike's for stolen travellers' cheques.'

Meadows glared at him, then, without a word, reached for the phone. Barlow strolled across to a chair and sat down.

'You know it's out of order.'

Meadows threw the phone down and turned on Barlow.

'Just what do you think you're doing, copper. Bursting in here . . . .' He broke off as a crash from upstairs indicated the policemen were taking their searches seriously. Meadows' face grew red with rage.

'Now you listen to me . . .'

'No.' Barlow fired the word like a bullet. 'You listen to me. I don't like you Meadows. I don't like anything about you. I don't like people who sit around in country houses while other people do the dirty work for them. You've always thought you were too big to touch, Meadows. Well, you aren't. This time it isn't going to happen to one of your side-kicks. It's going to happen to you.'

Before Meadows could answer, there was a knock at the door. The inspector's head appeared round it, followed by the inspector.

'Excuse me, sir,' he said to Barlow. 'But I thought you'd like to see these.' He opened his fist and showed Barlow two brown cheroots.

A broad grin spread across Barlow's face.

'Well, well.' He picked one up and sniffed it. . . . 'Marihuana. Dear me, Mr Meadows, I wouldn't have thought this was your style at all.'

Meadows snarled at him:

'They aren't mine. They belong to a friend.'

'So you say. But you know the law. This is your house. To permit drugs to be indulged in here is an offence. I'm going to have you charged with that. And I'm going to have you taken in – to the local station. That's right. The great Meadows is going to get stuck in a cell there. And you're going to be held.'

'You can't do that.'

'Oh yes I can.' Barlow spoke very softly, bending down with his face a few inches away. 'I can do just what I like. And you can shout and scream for your solicitor as long as you like. I'll decide when you get to see him. Because we're going to do you over, Meadows. I've got three men coming down from London. They're on their way at the moment. They're looking forward to questioning you, Meadows. One at a time. Round the clock. I reckon they'll keep it up for three days.'

'You can't do that.' Meadows stared back up at Barlow. 'You can't hold me on this charge. And you can't make the other one stick.'

'You could be right. I'll have a go at conspiracy, but you're quite right, we may not get enough evidence. But shall I tell you something? I don't care. I'm going to hold you anyway. And it isn't just me telling you this. I've been chatting to some very important people about you. And they don't care either. We may let you go after three days. And my instructions are that if you want to sue for wrongful arrest – then you're welcome. . . . Now on your feet.'

Meadows stood up slowly, and with the air of a man who had temporarily lost touch with reality, allowed the inspector to lead him out of the room. Barlow watched him being bundled into the car.

Suddenly a thought struck him and he went to the front door.

'Inspector?'

The inspector's head appeared at the window.

'Yes, sir?'

'Get on the radio and tell the Post Office to re-connect this phone, will you? I want to use it.'

20

Fenton pushed his chair back and got to his feet.

'I think that's the best way, Charles. We have no real evidence to go on, but it would be a salutary experience for that particular gentleman. And even politicians can benefit from salutary experiences.'

He picked up two photographs from the file in front of him and put them carefully inside an envelope. Before sealing it, he looked up at Barlow.

'You are sure that he played no direct part in this?'

'Positive. I don't think he had any concept of the nature of the operation, let alone its scale. On the other hand, he was perfectly prepared to go along with Meadows and one or two of the others in a scheme which he knew was intended to cause damage and possibly some loss of life. I think his idea was that anything along that line would help his call for strong leadership.'

Fenton nodded gently.

'He and his followers feel they have a particular gift for strong leadership, don't they?' He stuck down the flap. 'Well, let us sally forth, Charles. I am informed that we shall find our friend in a leather armchair in the bar of the club. That apparently is his regular practice. It isn't a club I normally take any pleasure in entering. But I have a feeling this time I am going to enjoy myself.'

As they pushed open the glass-fronted inside doors of the club, an attendant who looked as if he should have been retired at least twenty years earlier came slowly forward to meet them. Fenton looked around him with distaste at the gloomy, drab surroundings.

'You know, Charles, I can't think why anyone should ever come here voluntarily. I had lunch here about six months ago and the food is worse than the furniture. I think I must cancel my subscription.'

He turned to the attendant who was hovering uncertainly at his elbow.

'Is Mr Montague Wheeler in the club?'

'Yes, sir. You will find him in the bar, sir. His usual chair is just inside the door on the left.'

'Thank you.'

They walked into the bar and stood for a moment just inside the door.

'There he is,' said Fenton and walked across to where a disgruntled-looking man in a dark suit was glowering into a copy of the *Daily Telegraph*. Fenton coughed gently.

'Mr Wheeler?'

The newspaper was lowered, but apart from that the only response was a brusque nod of the head and a grunt. Fenton continued unperturbed.

'My name is Fenton. We have met on one or two occasions. This is my colleague, Mr Barlow. I apologise for troubling you, but we should be grateful for a moment of your time.'

Without waiting for an answer he drew back one of the shiny leather armchairs and sat down. Barlow did the same, first taking the precaution of beckoning to a waiter. He and Fenton gave their orders. Mr Wheeler, without too much prompting, agreed to take another large Scotch. Fenton sat in tranquil silence until the waiter returned with the drinks. As soon as he had gone,

Wheeler picked his up and drank half of it without ceremony. As he lowered it, he said: 'Well, what's it about? Haven't got all day, you know. Must get back to the House.'

'Oh, I'm sure you can spare us a moment, sir.' Fenton was being particularly silky. 'There is no division expected until ten.'

'I know that, man.' Wheeler disappeared into his whisky glass again. 'Just get on with it.'

'Excuse me. I'll leave this to my colleague.' Fenton reached into his pocket and pulled out the envelope. He gave it to Barlow, and strolled away to the bar.

Barlow took one of the photographs out of the envelope and slid it face upwards across the table. Wheeler's florid face turned chalk-white.

'Where did you get that?' The hoarse, barking voice was a whisper. Barlow leant across and retrieved the photograph. His voice was precise and icily cold.

'It is our business to have these things, Mr Wheeler. It is also our business to decide what to do with them when we get them. I have been persuaded *not* to take the action I should like to – direct action.'

Barlow turned over an evening edition paper lying on a nearby chair. The headlines were screaming with a garbled account of the encounter in Anglesey.

'I wanted to lock you up, Mr Wheeler. As a matter of fact, I still do.'

Wheeler stared at the newspaper, his eyes nearly bulging out of his head.

'I had nothing to do with that . . . I swear it . . .'

'I know that, Mr Wheeler. But your colleagues – those gentlemen whom you so happily encouraged in their little conspiracies – they had a great deal to do with it.'

Some of the colour began to come back to Wheeler's face.

'You can't prove it. You can't prove any of it.' He started to gain confidence as he heard his own denials. 'You come in here, into this club and throw your wild accusations about it . . . I'll have you up before the bar of the House . . . I'll . . .'

Barlow cut him off brutally.

'One more remark like that and I assure you that I'll have you up in the dock in a criminal court. The charge will be conspiracy. You are fortunate to escape it as it is.'

Barlow got to his feet and Fenton strolled over to them. 'Finished, Charles? Very well.'

They were about to move away but, casually, Fenton paused. 'You appreciate, Wheeler, that the Prime Minister has been informed. Your political future is his prerogative. But I'm a member of this club and I take it your resignation will be handed in tonight?'

Wheeler stared at him.

'I'm giving you a chance you don't deserve,' said Fenton gently. 'Do it tonight, or I'll be talking to the committee in the morning. Good night.'

Barlow gave a low whistle. 'A bit vicious, that parting shot, more my kind of trick.'

Fenton stopped in his tracks and looked at Barlow with an air of surprise.

'My dear Charles, as a civil servant I am expected to try and suffer fools, if not gladly, then with some degree of tolerance. I refuse point blank, however, to show the same courtesy to knaves.'

Barlow was saved the need to reply. The ancient retainer who had greeted them on their arrival materialised at their elbow. He addressed himself to Fenton.

'Excuse me, sir. Would your guest's name be Mr Barlow?'

'It is indeed', said Fenton, looking slightly taken aback. The retainer slowly creaked around until he was facing Barlow.

'There is a telephone call for you in the lobby, sir.'

He indicated a dark, wooden booth which bore a sharp resemblance to an upright coffin. Barlow nodded his thanks.

'Don't wait for me. It's probably Johnstone in Anglesey reporting on the tidying up. I'll see you tomorrow morning.'

'Good night Charles.'

'Good night.'

Barlow picked up the phone. But the voice was a strange one.

'Mr Barlow?'

'Yes.'

'My name is Llewellyn, Chief Constable of East Mercia. Mr Barlow, you will recall a report of yours concerning a possible miscarriage of justice in Pontrhyd. I have decided that the matter does merit an investigation. My committee has authorised me to ask you to take charge of it. I have spoken to the Home Office and they have agreed that you should do so.'

Barlow thought for a moment.

'Could you have a car to meet the nine o'clock from Paddington tomorrow morning?'

'Yes of course.'

'Good. I'll report to you tomorrow, sir. Good night.'

He put the phone down and then, with a grin, leafed through his notebook, found a number and dialled it. It rang for a while, then a faint voice, with a stammer, spelled out the number. With a shrug, Barlow put the receiver back. He could give her the news after he got back – over dinner – or, preferably, after it.